A cow boy in Paris

# A COW BOY IN PARIS.

UNEXPECTED LOVE

*BY     J.MERRICK PALMER*

J. M Palmer

Copyright © 2022, All rights reserved. VL Sparks Library of Congress RE. No TXu 2-297-340 All Rights Reserved Publisher VL Sparks

A cow boy in Paris

**Printed by Amazon
Available from Amazon.com and other retail outlets.
Available from Kindle and bookstore**

J. M Palmer

**Dedication**

**I dedicate this book to diverse people who are unable to be who they are inside due to their circumstances.**

A cow boy in Paris

# Chapter 1

As usual, the train station was busy for a weekday at six a.m. as Amaury walked to a spot on the far side, opposite the ticket counter. Waiting and watching had seen a target of interest in the past few days. He was not a Frenchman, nor a European for that matter. The man, whom he'd named, 'Cowboy,' had come into his part of the city for whatever reason, and Amaury let himself be seen by the man here and there, just out of reach, this past week; a café here, a shop there, just enough to pique the man's interest. He'd decided today was the day he would make his move. He was in charge of the game. That's the way it was.

The man had to be from the American West. Someplace like Texas, Wyoming, or Montana. Wasn't that the way it was in American Cinema? And he wore expensive clothes, mostly cowboy boots, tight western jeans, and a shiny new Rolex. His 'Cowboy' would pay good money.

Amaury didn't have to wait around long. His 'Cowboy' came rushing up to the ticket counter line, and Amaury quickly got into line just behind him. He didn't need a ticket. He had a rail pass, but he wanted to let the American know he'd noticed him looking and tease him just a bit.

Rawlin had overslept, which he rarely ever did, and knew he would miss the first train to Rouen, where he was working, not far from Paris. Even though he was just a plain cowboy from the Texas panhandle, he loved this city. He'd opted to stay here and deal with the commute every day instead of staying in Rouen, quickly paying for a ticket. He just needed to bite the bullet and get a pass, but not today, running late as he was. Turning quickly, he ran smack into the person standing behind him. "Oh, I'm sorry...." He stopped mid-sentence. It was the same young man again. He sure did get around this city, making Rawlin very nervous. "Excuse me." He slid past him, unable to avert his eyes. Rawlin shook it off, jogging to catch the train.

Behind him, Amaury wore a satisfied grin and waited for the 'Cowboy' to turn and look back. He didn't even make it five seconds before he did. Amaury gave him one of his best seductive looks, then watched the man slip onto the train just before it departed.

Rawlin cursed himself for looking back. "Damn it," he mumbled. He couldn't help himself. He watched the young man until he could no longer see him in the station. Was that how it worked between two men? He sure wouldn't know, but he did know that no other men would keep eye contact longer than a good few seconds before looking away. Rawlin pulled out a magazine from his briefcase to occupy his mind for the short trip trying to think of something else.

Amaury was thrilled with what had happened. He had planted the idea in the cowboy's head. It was perfect. The man would think of him on and off, throughout the day, now. Good money and fun were coming his way.

The man was handsome, indeed, though you could tell that he sure didn't think so. His short brown hair was neat, with curls at the ends, and a clean shadow of a beard adorned his face. But it was his sky blue eyes that first got Amaury's attention—those eyes could melt anyone.

The other information of the day was that now Amaury knew the man's destination, and Amaury would make sure that he was back at the station whenever the trains from Rouen arrived. He'd give the guy at least four hours to do whatever he was doing in Rouen and then come back.

Amaury looked at the arrival times and then planned what to do in the meantime. Hmmm, how about going out to Versailles? He hadn't been out there for a time, and he so loved it. Amaury could see a train departing in moments by looking at the schedule. He made his way through the station to the train. Fifteen minutes later, it left the station.

## Chapter 2

Amaury's world consisted of Paris's city and surrounding areas accessed by rails of some kind. That's what he did, work the rails and the city. He had a strange love/hate affair with the rails of Paris for the past three years.

Amaury pulled out a tattered paperback from his jacket pocket to get comfortable in the seat. A worn copy of 'Dune, read many times, would suffice during

He hurried off the train and headed for the Chateau. The train pulled into the Versailles Rive Gauche station just east of Amaury's destination. Before the crowds gathered, early morning was the best time to see this marvel. Note that on this particular weekday, there wouldn't be many tourists around.

As he approached the Chateau, its massiveness still amazed Amaury. He had been here many times, and still, this home of the Sun King, a young Louis XIV, was a favorite of his. The young king had chosen the sun as his emblem. Amaury used a student pass he'd lifted off someone to get into the grounds for free. He used to steal to get by but quickly found out that his looks were the way to get by in the city, which was much more manageable. He headed for the Grand Apartment or Abundant Salon and others dedicated to heavenly bodies. The details of the place, and the care put into the rooms, were without description, and Amaury loved them.

As Amaury toured the salons, he entered the hall of mirrors. Walking by, he drew lots of attention from female and male admirers. It had always been this way for him and used to be an annoyance. Quickly learning how to use his looks for power, and now, for survival, his dark wavy hair brushed his shoulders, his face symmetrical, and his cheeks chiseled, yet soft and androgynous, and why he attracted both sexes. He could use the cheeks for wonderful pouts to get his way, and his dark eyes surrounded by long lashes that, when batted, got many favors.

His body was tall and willowy, and the eyes were dark and knowing. Much more wisdom was in the eyes for the age that Amaury was. He was sexy, and he knew it.

After spending a couple of hours in residence, Amaury bought bread and juice from a vendor and sat on a garden bench to enjoy them. The landscaping was just as impressive as the residence, and the perfect green and color placement looked like a canvas, making Amaury want to sketch them. It was very peaceful and relaxing here, and maybe that's why he liked coming here.

After eating, he walked until he found an out-of-the-way hedgerow and took a nap under it, unseen. And when he woke, it was time to go back to the rail station to wait for the cowboy.

## Chapter 3

Rawlin had had a hectic day chock full of meetings with supervisors, company heads, and paperwork to set up the job of surveying for fiber-optic cable installed under some historic buildings in Rouen.

    Rawlin had been abroad for some time now. He knew that he had to go back to Texas one day but wouldn't stay long. Depression would come back. It always did. That's why, since he'd left there years ago, and he'd only been back a handful of times. It was tough enough over here.

Praying for jobs in far-away places to keep coming in, where no one knew the personal story of Rawlin Jones, this job came along after three years of overseas work, then been offered this supervisory position, and gained a salary that had increased rapidly. At least he didn't have to worry about money.

    As the train got closer to the station, Rawlin thought about Paris. He loved its history, food, traditions, and people. Even though many Americans mistook their bluntness for rudeness, Rawlin didn't. It was somehow refreshing to him.

The young man crept into his mind again. He had, on and off again, during the day. Rawlin had seen him around the city, here and there, and there was just something charming about him, more than the others. Sure, he was beautiful, but so were others in Paris. And what had happened earlier at the train station between the two of them? What had it meant?

When the cowboy didn't arrive by six o'clock, Amaury became annoyed. He might as well busy himself by looking for action elsewhere. He began to cruise the station, and he didn't have to wait long. An English businessman met his eye, winked, and headed into the closest toilet. Amaury followed. It would be quick, easy money.

The train was right on schedule. As it got closer to the station, Rawlin got more anxious, and when it finally pulled to a stop, he had butterflies in his stomach.

Stop being ridiculous! He was just a kid! But would he be around?

Rawlin sat next to the door to be one of the first to get off. But as he stepped out, he looked around. The young man was not around. Disappointment weighed heavily on Rawlin as he walked. What the hell did he expect to do if he was there anyway? Oh yes, he'd been looking for a long time, but only looking, never daring to do anything about these feelings. He walked through the station, out toward the street.

After he'd passed, Amaury came out from around the corner where he'd been watching the cowboy. He now followed at a safe distance, knowing the man would probably look around just once more before he left the station. It worked just as he'd planned, too. Rawlin, still disappointed, turned around to look for the young man.

As soon as their eyes met, Rawlin jerked his head back around. Feeling like a fool, he rushed out of the station.

The blood was pounding in his ears, and it was hard to breathe.

Rawlin walked along a few feet and then leaned on the wall, waiting.

A cow boy in Paris

Amaury was amused watching the cowboy almost stumble as he'd been caught, looking back for him. He'd be strolling or waiting on the street. And he was. When Amaury began walking his way, Rawlin got the nerve to say, "Salut," in his broad Texas accent. Amaury stopped and looked at him. He decided to answer in English since the cowboy had spoken in French. It was, after all, a mind game.

When the man just looked down at the ground, saying nothing more, Amaury began to walk away. Rawlin stuttered after him.

"I could go for an espresso or something. Want to join me?" Amaury stopped, smiled to himself, and walked back to the cowboy, standing just inches from his face. Rawlin got nervous and stepped back.

"Oui, an espresso and…." Amaury stepped so close their lips almost touched. Rawlin, intoxicated by the guy's looks, froze for a moment. God, he smelled good, but what the hell was he doing? Was he crazy? He took a couple of side steps, looking back at the ground. He held up his hand, looking at the guy.

"I'm sorry." He hurried to the curb, hailed a taxi, and was gone before Amaury could object. Just great! He had scared the man off. He went back inside the station to cruise again. He was confused. The man had seemed interested enough to ask him to an espresso yet, run away. Oh well, they'd see one another again. Amaury vowed to make sure they would.

Amaury went on to have a good evening, anyway. He put the money he'd earned in his shoe, found an out-of-the-way bench, curled up, and slept.

Amaury decided to stay out of the cowboy's way for the next two days. Leave him hungry. Make him miss and yearn for him more.

Rawlin was hungry indeed, hungry for more. He had kicked himself back to the hotel for running away. And to make things worse, the young man was nowhere to be found. Perhaps he'd never see him again. Before he'd been a scared idiot, the Frenchman had been everywhere. It was distressing. Rawlin tried to concentrate on his work.

On the third day, Rawlin came walking into the terminal heading for his train when he caught a glimpse of the guy about a hundred yards away. He was getting on the same train that Rawlin was about to take. No, that couldn't be. He was losing his mind now, seeing the guy because he wanted to so badly.

Amaury had thought this plan out carefully. He boarded the train taking a seat at the back of the car, facing the passengers who were boarding. He pulled out the novel, pretending to read.

Rawlin's heart was practically beating out of his chest by the time he boarded the train. He took a seat facing the guy, not by choice, but it was one of the only ones left when he got up the nerve to get on the train. He had butterflies in his stomach again and scolded himself. Get a grip, Jones! Okay, he wouldn't look at the guy. He just wouldn't. Don't start it up again. Be a man. But what was that? He pulled a report he was studying out of his briefcase to look over. He tried hard to concentrate as the train was about to pull out of the station. Amaury watched the passengers out the window and then looked at his book. He wouldn't give the cowboy any attention just yet. Only when the train was out of the station did Amaury look.

Across the car, Rawlin couldn't stand it any longer and looked up to see the boy watching him. He could have sworn he had a slight smirk on his face. Damn it! Embarrassed, he looked back down at his report. When he finally had the nerve to look again, the guy was gone!

Amaury was playing with the cowboy's mind. He was good at this cat and mouse game, and he was always the cat. He had moved into the next car when the American wasn't looking. He watched from the other vehicle as the cowboy turned around to try and find him. He sat back, looking so sad and disappointed.

Rawlin turned around and slumped down a little. He suddenly felt so old and alone. He leaned his head down, closed his eyes, and kept telling himself that he could not do the things he desired to do. Amaury saw his chance. It seemed the man had drifted off to sleep. He entered the car again, making sure to brush lightly against the cowboy's arm as he passed. Rawlin warned of pickpockets, sat up in alarm. He was staring up into the deep brown eyes of the young man. Who kept on walking into the car in front of them. Amaury went into the car ahead of them looked back with his little satisfied smirk as the door closed behind him. Rawlin laughed at the teasing.

At Rouen, as much as he hated it, Rawlin had to get to work, or he'd miss his meeting. And while Rawlin was at work, Amaury walked into the town where he meets a boy around his age, with whom he spends the afternoon, in bed, just for himself, no pay. He'd have to leave the guy behind, for now, knowing they'd see one another again. But he was at the train station from five o'clock on, not sure which afternoon train cowboy would take.

It was the seven o'clock train, and Amaury decided to sit two cars away from his target this time. After they arrived, he made sure that the cowboy got off first and followed him at a leisurely pace. This time, Rawlin was aware that the guy was following him. Amaury stopped halfway to the street, posing against a column in the walkway. He wanted to be sure the cowboy was interested tonight. And when Rawlin looked back, he almost missed the young man. He smiled and gestured for Amaury to come with him. Amaury did, and without a word, they headed for the street where Rawlin hailed a cab, opened the door for the beautiful Parisian, who slid into the car, followed by Rawlin. "Ladida Hotel, please," he told the driver and then sat back, and the ride continued in silence.

In the night, no matter how many times Amaury had seen Paris, he was taken in by how romantic the place was and understood why people always wished to come here. He slid up onto the edge of his seat as the Tower Eiffel appeared in between the buildings. Amaury smiled and sighed. He was like a little boy.

"Magnificent!" He pointed to the famous landmark and then looked at the cowboy, then back to the tower until it was no longer in view. He sat back in the seat. Up close, his beauty was even more stunning.

Amaury was pleased with things so far.

At the hotel, Amaury hopped out while Rawlin paid the driver, and they walked through the eloquent lobby and into the elevator. Inside, Rawlin didn't have to look over at the boy to know he was checking him out.

The doors open on the third floor, and Amaury followed Rawlin down the hall to the last room, where he got a card key from his wallet. Amaury waited, looking around as the man slid the card into the lock. Nothing happened. He tried three more times, and still, it did not work. Rawlin sighed and looked at Amaury.

"These damned cards! Whatever happened to keys? Keys were good and simple." Amaury was amused and smiled. He held out his hand, into which Rawlin put the card—sliding the card into the lock, the door opened on the first try. Amaury handed the card back to Rawlin, his eyes laughing. "Thanks. I hate those cards." They walked into the room, and Rawlin shut the door behind them.

The room had a kitchenette, parlor, balcony, large master bedroom with a full bath. Rawlin could care less. All he expected of a room was a soft, clean bed and a clean shower. The company paid for it, so whatever.

Now what? He looked at Amaury, who was waiting. He was surprised at what he did instead of explaining what he wanted. "Um, make yourself at home, okay? Oh, you do speak English, right?" Amaury nodded. "Good, 'cause my French is terrible." He pulled off his jacket, hanging it on a barstool. "I'm gonna change clothes. Be right back."

Rawlin walked into the bedroom, shutting the door behind him, leaving Amaury to his own devices. He looked around the place. There was a mini-bar. He'd start by making himself a Cosmopolitan.

Rawlin had changed into a pair of loose-faded jeans and a blue-grey polo shirt, which he left un-tucked. He'd taken off his boots and went barefoot. Checking his breath and, on the way out of the bathroom, caught sight of himself in the mirror. He stopped. God, he looked too old! He ruffled his hair, trying to look more casual, calm, and younger. He took a deep breath. "What the hell are you doing, Jones? Geez." One more breath, and he opened the bedroom door and came out. The young man, jacket removed, was sitting on the couch, his feet on the coffee table, and drink in hand. "Take your shoes off if you're going to put them on the furniture, will ya?"

Amaury wasn't sure he was serious until he looked at the man's face.

Amaury slipped out of his worn brown-laced shoes and put his feet up again. "Thank you." Rawlin just stood there, wringing his hands. He hadn't been this nervous in a long, long time. Amaury took a drink. "A drink, yeah, a drink sounds like a wonderful idea right about now." Rawlin fixed himself a glass.

Amaury liked his accent. He was pretty sure he was a Texan now.

Rawlin fixed himself a whiskey and coke, practically drinking it in one gulp and fixing himself another. He walked to the wall leaning on it, and had to ask a question. "How old are you, anyway? Are you old enough to drink that?" He pointed to Amaury's glass. Amaury knew he'd ask. He usually was. He told them what they wanted to hear.

"Twenty-One," he lied. It came easily. They didn't want to know if he was under-aged. Rawlin was studying his face. Amaury looked back.

"Come on, kid, I'm not that stupid. How old are you? It's a simple question." Amaury usually stuck to his lies, no matter what, once told, but somehow he didn't want to lie to this man. He sighed and said that he was nineteen. Rawlin downed his second drink. "That the truth?" He kept his eye on the boy, who nodded. "Thank you. I believe you." Amaury finished his drink in a final swallow. "What's that you are drinking? I'll fix another one. Cosmo?"

"Oui Cosmopolitan." He handed his glass to the American and then pulled his legs up onto the couch. He wanted to hear his sexy accent more.

"You want more juice or more fire in it?" Amaury was confused by his words, not entirely understanding what he meant. Rawlin explained. "Fire is the alcohol, baby."

"More fire, then." Rawlin nodded. Oh, god, he had! Had he just called this boy, baby?

Rawlin handed the drink to Amaury, who noticed his hand was shaking. Rollin still didn't sit down. He leaned on the wall instead.

"I've seen you around the city, you know, lots of places. You get around, don't you?" He took another big drink. Amaury put his feet back on the table.

"Oui, I ride the rails of Paris." He shrugged and drank more.

The cowboy's hands were shaking more now. He was more nervous than Amaury realized. He might have to take charge of things if the cowboy didn't know what to do. It wouldn't be the first time.

Rawlin finished the drink and poured another lighter on the whiskey this time. He had to stay clear-headed.

While Rawlin put ice into the glass, Amaury decided to take it to the next level. He came up behind Rawlin and slid his arms around his hips, his hands ending up on his groin. Rawlin spun around, facing the boy, drink splashing on both of them.

"Hey, hey, wait a minute. Just wait a minute." These were the words his mouth said, but his eyes told Amaury this was not what he wanted, so Amaury leaned in, grinding his hips against the man's as he brushed his lips with a kiss. Rawlin felt light-headed. He quickly sat his drink down and took Amaury by the wrists. "What the hell are you doing?" He forced Amaury to back up. "Just wait a minute here, okay?" Amaury was confused. He sat on the arm of the couch, watching the man. Why had he brought him up to his hotel room only to refuse him?

"The age of consent is sixteen, cowboy. No problems." Rawlin ignored him, picked up his drink, and finished it, so Amaury did the same with his and sat down again. He pulled his knees up to his chest, and the two just looked at one another for a few minutes. Amaury couldn't read the man. He made a move.

"Come sit, at least." Rawlin nodded and sat in the chair nearest to the boy but not on the couch. That was too close. Rawlin began to babble from nervousness and the whiskey.

"Yeah, I've seen you everywhere. At café's sipping coffee alone, or on the Seine, everywhere I see you. And in the train station, too, I see you."

Amaury just listened to him. The nervousness was sweet on him. He was just probably one of those married men who'd always wanted a man or been curious about what it would be. They traveled far away from home, and in a foreign country, maybe they'd try it out, and no one would know, especially the wife and family. Amaury looked at his ring finger. Yes, there was still a faint tan line there, where a ring once was. Amaury didn't know that the Wedding ring had only recently come off. "Have you been following me?" Amaury shrugged.

"I watch you sometimes, Oui. So?" Rawlin knew it! He hoped this kid wasn't a psycho or a little blackmailer or something. That would just be his luck.

"So you have followed me before today." Amaury just smiled at him and seductively ran a hand through his hair. It made Rawlin take in a sharp breath.

"Today, I follow you." He crossed his long, lean legs, his eyes twinkling at Rawlin, who melted. He couldn't think clearly, or was it the drink? He would just keep on talking for now.

"I'm here for work. It's nice here." At this, Amaury scowled, shaking his head.

"London is nice. Los Angeles might be nice, but Paris, um, nice is not the word you say…oxon moron, I think? Two words that don't agree?" Rawlin told him it was an oxymoron. "Paris is the essence of life! We have world history, romance, and art, and people of creativity!" He held up a fist.

"I'm assuming that you are from Paris, then?" Rawlin leaned forward in his chair, feeling a little less nervous.

"Oui, close by." It was best not to tell anyone the exact details of him. "You, are you a real Texas cowboy?" Rawlin laughed more easily now. The drinks were catching up to him, for sure.

"Yeah, I guess I am."

Amaury stretched out on the couch, lying on his side, resting his head on his arm, posing for the man. He ran his hand down his long, lean side. Rawlin kept on talking, but his eyes followed Amaury's hand.

"My name is Rawlin Jones." Oh, geez! Why did he use his real name and his LAST name? What an idiot, again.

"Rolling? Is not a strange name in your Texas?" Rawlin laughed.

"No, not rolling like a wheel. Raaaawlin. You hear it?"

"Rawlin. Yes, I see. Is a good name for my cow boy."

Rawlin liked the fact that he'd said, 'my' cowboy. It was sexy, too. Everything this kid did was sexy. Amaury licked his lips with his tongue.

"Um, yeah. So, what's your name? Some cute French name that fits you?" Oh, man, why did he say that? It was stupid! Amaury rolled on his back, arms above his head exposing half of his stomach. He knew Rawlin would like it, and he did.

"Amaury is my name. I don't know if it fits me, but it is me." He ran his hands down his stomach and onto his legs, with Rawlin practically drooling.

"Is that your real name, kid? I told you mine, though I probably shouldn't have."

"It is my name for real, Rooolllliiinnnggg," he said, mispronouncing it on purpose. It made Rawlin laugh. Amaury loved his deep laugh. "I am no 'kid.''

"You got a surname, Amaury?" Rawlin watched the smile fade away, and a sad, lost look replaced it. He rolled over to face away from the cowboy.

"Non. Its m'ont jete', je vous ont dit' Amaury could see that Rawlin didn't understand, so he translated, 'No. My family threw me away.' Amaury didn't roll back over, just talked into the cushions of the couch. "Was not acceptable that I like males. They say to stop or leave the family, so I must go."

As naïve as it was of Rawlin, he wasn't sure that the young man was gay until that moment. How sad to be disowned for being gay.

Amaury rolled back over, looking at him. "Never pity me. I am on my own since sixteen, and I manage well." He scowled at Rawlin, knowing he was feeling sorry for him.

"Yeah, I'll bet you do pretty good, looking like that." Well, fuck, he'd said that out loud, what he was thinking. Amaury's face softened a little.

"You, with your beautiful blue eyes, and tight cowboy jeans, would not do so bad, yourself, Rawlin Jones." He winked at

Rawlin, which made him blush and want just to pass out right then and there. No one had ever said anything like that to him, especially a male. He knew this might be the right time to ask about money, for Amaury's time. It would be awkward. How should he do it?

"I don't know how to bring this up, but I know you have to take care of yourself, and you are with me now, and hey," he suddenly had an idea, "I'll bet you're hungry. Want to eat something? I'm hungry." He looked at the clock and forgot about the money.

Amaury gave him a suggestive smile and moved closer to Rawlin. He knew what his cowboy wanted.

"Oui, for you, Cheri." He moved a hand down Rawlin's chest before he could do anything. He looked at Rawlins very apparent arousal.

Rawlin suddenly felt naked and afraid. He turned away from Amaury and paced the room. Getting out of the room seemed like a good idea.

"If we hurry, I think we can get something to eat here at the hotel before the kitchen closes. Come on. I'll get my boots. You get your shoes on. I'll buy you supper and then…." Rawlin went to get his boots from the bedroom. When he returned, Amaury was standing by the barstools. "Let's go."

Rawlin grabbed the card key, and they headed down to the lobby and the restaurant. The host gave them a very odd look, led them to a table, and said that they were serving a limited menu because the kitchen was soon closing. Rawlin told the man that was fine with them. The man gave Amaury a stern look and then walked away. Amaury gave him a fake smile and then looked at the menu.

"The cuisine is excellent here." The waitress came around to take a drink order of two cokes on ice.

"You've been here before, with other men?" Somehow, this hurt Rawlins feelings a little, as ridiculous as it sounded. The waitress brought them some bread, from which Amaury tore a piece off, speaking with his mouth full.

"Oui, a few times, I have worked here. The beds are very soft, too, Cheri." He took another bite of bread as Rawlin looked around nervously to see if anyone overheard the suggestive remark. "The help, they know me. They don't like me to come." He shrugged and ate more of the bread. Rawlin could see just how hungry he was now. He tore off some of the bread, too.

"So, Amaury, do you work anyplace else or go to school or something, you know, besides this?" He just couldn't call it what it was, so Amaury did.

"You mean to have sex with men? I sketch too, but mainly I hustle. It's a fine job for me to do, as you say, with looks." He sipped his coke.

"I guess that's great if you are happy and safe." Both men reached for bread simultaneously, and their hands touched. It was like an electric shock to Rawlin, who pulled back his hand

"What is to be happy anyway? I don't believe we know, sometimes. Perhaps to find love would make me have this happiness."

The waitress took their order of sandwiches so that the cook could shut down the grill and some wine. She soon returned with it, and soon, they were the only ones left in the place except for the waitress.

"Yes, love can make you happy, Amaury." Amaury pouted. This man was married. He was suddenly jealous, but why?

"So, you have this happiness back in Texas, my cowboy? I figure you for married and wandering, here." Rawlin looked a little white when he said this. He rubbed his ring finger sadly.

"Yes, I was married, and my wife, pregnant with my baby girl whenever she died." Rawlin's face said that he spoke the truth. The revelation was unfortunate, indeed. "I just had the heart to take off my wedding ring a couple of months ago."

"I am sorry for you, Rawlin. What happens to her and the baby?"

Rawlin didn't know why he was even talking about this to this stranger of Paris. He never spoke about it to anyone, but he did tonight.

"A drunk driver crashed into her car, head-on. They say she died instantly."

Amaury was so touched that this man shared with him about his life. No one ever cared to do that with him. They just had sex; he got paid and then left.

"This must be the hardest thing ever, to lose a love." Rawlin sipped his drink and nodded his head. They ate in silence for a few moments, and then Amaury told Rawlin something he never talked about, either.

"My older brother, Arnaud, is lost to me. He jumps on the rails. Ir's still very hard to think of it. Is the same as you, I think, these feelings?"

Were you two very close?" Rawlin wondered if this were true.

"Very much so. I miss every moment of my day and nights." He looked so sad and small to Rawlin, once again. One moment, he was a man, the next, a boy. "Rawlin?" Rawlin looked him in the eye. "At least you can say that you did once in love. Not everyone can say so. Some never will say this."

Rawlin let what this nineteen-year-old said sink in as he tried to eat a few more bites. Had he ever been in love? Yes, he had loved Leslie, and they'd been best friends. They could talk about anything, but was there passion between them? No, there never had been. They'd met in college, and everyone had expected them to get married, and so they had. Amaury watched Rawlin, who was very deep in thought and sad. When he looked up, Rawlin brushed the thoughts away and smiled.

"You sure like watching people, doncha?" Amaury smiled, giggled, and nodded. Then he got serious again.

"You learn much of people just to watch them. Do you know the real person? If they know you are watching, it is not them sometimes, but if they don't know, true personality is present, I think."

"Ah, but not you, unless you want to let someone inside. You are pretty good at that. You hide your emotions when you need to. You learn that doing your work?"

"Oui." That was very true. Amaury was an expert at it.

The two of them ate the rest of their meal in silence, and then they shared a rich cream cake before Rawlin signed for the bill, and they headed out of the restaurant.

Amaury wasn't sure whether to go or stay. He looked to Rawlin for an answer. Rawlin wasn't sure until that moment, either. He handed Amaury the card key, and they headed for the elevator. When the doors closed, Amaury leaned over and kissed Rawlin on the cheek.

"Merci, beau coupe, for the meal and the company. Is pleasant with you, cowboy." Rawlin blushed a little.

"Well, thanks. I've enjoyed it, too."

The two men walked down to the room, and the door opened on the first try for Amaury, and Rawlin groaned. When Amaury opened the door, Rawlin asked him to shut it.

"I'm gonna get this damned door open right now. Give me that damned card." Amaury giggled and handed him the card. Rawlin carefully inserted it into the lock. Nothing. He tried two more times before handing the card to Amaury. It opened on the first try. "Well, son of a bitch!" Amaury gave him a little, 'ha-ha,' Rawlin slapped his ass and shooed him into the room. "Just get into the room, smartass." They were both laughing hard, now. It felt good to both, to genuinely laugh like this. Neither had done so in a long time.

Amaury laid the card key on the bar and waited for Rawlin to tell him what came next. The trouble was Rawlin still wasn't sure. They both walked into the bedroom, where Rawlin took off his western boots.

"Got to have a wake-up call." Rawlin sat on the bed and rang the office for an eight o'clock call, and then he hung up. "That's as late as I can sleep, sorry."

"I never stay for the morning." Rawlin looked back at him. The kid meant what he said, so Rawlin didn't ask him why. Now he would have to figure out why he invited this beautiful young man into his bedroom.

"You do wear underwear, don't you?" Amaury looked at him oddly and then nodded. "Undress, but keep them on, and about the money...I don't know what you need from me." Amaury put a finger to his lips and shushed the man, though he didn't know why. "Be right back." Rawlin hurried into the bathroom and shut the door. He leaned against it, breathing hard again.

## A cow boy in Paris

"Okay, old man, you have a beautiful, willing young man in your bedroom, so just take it easy." He undressed to his black boxer-briefs, brushed his teeth, peed, and then came out. Rawlin was just crazy, he thought.

Amaury had undressed to red micro briefs and then sat on the bed, leaning against the headboard. He drew his long legs up to one side and waited for his cowboy to emerge from the bathroom. He reached over and turned on the stereo to some soft house music. Whenever he looked up, Rawlin stood in the doorway looking at him.

"Oh, you turned on some music. I like music. That's good." Amaury looked at the stereo and then back at Rawlin. He was pleased with what he saw. The slight belly that he had was endearing to Amaury. Rawlin couldn't move. He was thinking how he'd lost his mind, being here like this. For all of these years, he'd looked away and restrained himself from even thinking about doing something with a man. Yet, here he was with a beautiful young man in his bedroom.

Amaury put on a show for him, too. He stretched out his long body, and his long hair swung forward into his face. Amaury was still so touched by the man's shyness. He patted the bed next to him. Rawlin sighed and slowly walked to the bed. He turned down the light next to the bed and turned down the covers.

What the hell was he supposed to do now? He looked at Amaury, and then his eyes stopped on the television. "You watch much TV? I don't. Just seem to work all the time. Yep, I work, eat, and sleep, I guess. That's my life." Oh, Rawlin, just shut up! You sound like an old fool just babbling on and on.

"Television is not much of my life either. I am riding my rails and working."

Rawlin asked him to turn off the music, and he turned on the TV. The English subtitles were already on at the bottom of the screen. He flipped through the channels trying to find something interesting. He laughed whenever he saw John Wayne's face come across the screen. Amaury's face lit up. "Cowboys!" Rawlin laid the remote on the bed between them. "John Wayne is the best cowboy, oui?"

Rawlin looked at him, smiling and nodding. He seemed about twelve years old.

"Yes, he is, indeed."

It was odd indeed, to Amaury, but sweet, too. He grabbed a pillow and put it at the end of the bed, then lay down with his feet at the head of the bed. He knew it would be hard for the man not to be turned on by looking at him this way.

Rawlin, who'd been getting sleepy, opened his eyes again, looking down at the beautiful body lying next to him. Looking at Amaury was making him get aroused again, so he pulled the covers up to his chest. Amaury knew why and tried not to smile. He turned and looked back at Rawlin a couple of times.

Amaury's body begged to be touched, but Rawlin couldn't allow himself that pleasure. That was enough for now. It's a massive step for Rawlin. Let it be. He closed his eyes just for a moment to refocus on what was happening on the TV.

Amaury watched the whole movie, and then, as the credits rolled, he turned over to look at his cowboy, who had fallen asleep. Aw, how sweet

He trusted Amaury enough to sleep with him. Now he could check out the cowboy a bit closer without making him so nervous. He moved up to the head of the bed, lying on his side to see. He was very handsome and a bit rugged, which was perfect. He seemed like a good man, a gentleman who wore his heart on his sleeve. He wanted to do the right thing. He was also very naïve for a man of his age, whatever that might be. Amaury guessed maybe early to mid-thirties. Amaury could have easily robbed him. On the nightstand was his wallet, with cash sticking out the side. And the Rolex was on the bar in the main room. It would fetch an excellent price, and Amaury wouldn't have to hustle for a while. But he wouldn't do that to this one. He would have to warn Rawlin to be more careful with other boys and be less trusting.

After going to the bathroom, Amaury turned the volume down on the TV and slid under the covers. He wanted to feel their bodies touching before he left, so he moved to Rawlin and laid down next to his body, rubbing his hand down Rawlin's chest, caressing it gently.

Rawlin, who was in a dead sleep, woke with a start and roughly shoved Amaury away.

"What the hell do you think you're doing to me? Geez! Did I ask you to do anything to me?" He pushed Amaury a little further away.

Amaury got up and began to get dressed. He spoke in French quickly and angrily, so Rawlin had no idea what he was saying. He felt terrible now. "Wait a minute. Where are you going?" Amaury gave him a 'go-to hell' look, found his jeans, pulled them on, grabbed his shirt, and headed out the bedroom door. "No, wait! Don't leave, Amaury. That's not what I want." He jumped out of bed to follow the boy. Amaury was already near the door, shoes in his hand. Rawlin hurried over, stepping in front of the boy, who was more upset now than angry. He refused to look Rawlin in the eyes. If he did, he might begin to cry. He wouldn't do it. He was hurt. He'd been beaten by men before, but this was a different kind of hurt. A beating would have been better. A man had never rejected him, and it would not start now.

"Get out of my way, you scared, confused little cowboy," he spoke in French, but Rawlin understood. He was almost in a panic. He knew if he let the boy leave, he'd never see him again. He didn't move.

"Please look at me." Amaury slowly raised his head. "I'm sorry. You just surprised me. I'm very sorry. Please, I don't want you to leave."

Amaury studied his face. Rawlins's eyes pleaded for forgiveness and were full of remorse. Amaury sat his shoes on the floor, and they walked back into the bedroom together. This time, Amaury left his jeans on and climbed under the covers. Rawlin wanted to clarify what he wanted so that Amaury would be clear.

"Just sleep with me, okay? That's all I can do, okay? Just stay."

Amaury realized that the man was serious. He just wanted him to sleep with him.

"Is fine, to just sleep. Don't push me away again."

"I can't believe I pushed you like that. I've never done anything like that."

Amaury was shaking his head. That wasn't what he meant.

"No, not that hurt. I've been beaten and hit, and I felt hurt. Do you understand?"

He patted his heart. Now Rawlin did understand what he meant.

"I hurt your feelings, and for that, I am sorry." Amaury cocked his head and gave a weak little smile. He was appreciative of this genuine apology to a hustler from the streets like himself. Amaury got situated on his side of the bed and closed his eyes. But Rawlin was curious now.

"Does that happen to you very often, getting beat on, I mean?" Amaury opened his eyes and pulled the covers down to his chest. He thought back to some of the times that it had happened.

"It happens, Rawlin. I'm hit or slapped. They pay for me so they think they can do anything to my person. But I am smart, you see. I think my way out of most situations as this." He closed his eyes again, but Rawlin persisted.

"But how do you know that one of these guys won't go too far, be a psycho or something and kill you?" Amaury laughed. This guy watched too much TV.

"It's in the eyes, mostly, I think. Your eyes are beautiful, as I said, but they are, how you say, um, wholesome?" Rawlin sighed. It figured. He might as well have a target painted on his back! That's why he'd chosen.

"You mean plain or boring. I looked like a plain, naïve, easy mark."

"Rawlin Jones, yes, your looks and the smart dress got my attention, but I would not still be here, in your bed, if you were plain and boring, Cheri." He winked again. Rawlin thanked him with a bit of a smile and settled in.

"Sweet dreams, Amaury." It was what his family had always said to one another at bedtime, as corny as it seemed. He turned his back to the boy, closed his eyes, and soon, he was back asleep. Soon, Amaury slept

## Chapter 4

Up just before the Sun, Amaury went to the bathroom and got dressed. He found a notepad and pen on the desk. He left Rawlin a note on the bar, next to the Rolex. He then slipped on his shoes and headed out the door.

He got a few nasty looks from the staff in the lobby, but he walked out, head held high. He walked to the bakery just a few blocks away.

When he got closer, he saw a man headed the same way. Great! Now he would get a complimentary breakfast as he arrived at the bakery just as the man did, who held open the door for Amaury.

"After you." He had a heavy German accent. Amaury gave him his best pout and shook his head. Amaury was drooling over the food. The man looked at him again. It was going to work, as always. The men of Paris were always buying him breakfast on their way to work. He just stood outside the place, ogling at the goodies inside, and whenever he came out of the business, handing Amaury some change. "Go in and get yourself something to eat, son. You're thin enough as is." Amaury thanked him and went inside the bakery. Amaury only got a croissant and a coffee. The fresh bread tasted good.

The jarring of the wake-up call jarred Rawlin from the bed. In a great mood and guilt-free, he rolled over to look at his beautiful boy and then remembered Amaury's comment about leaving before morning, and the beautiful boy was gone. Damn it. Rawlin was so disappointed.

In the shower, he thought about the Amaury. He was like a painting come to life or something. Perhaps it was something else. Rawling suddenly panicked. What if the guy robbed him?

Quickly drying off, he was relieved to see his wallet still lying next to the bed, bills sticking out. He checked. It was all there.

After quickly dressing, he headed into the parlor. The Rolex was on the bar. There was a note.

"La s'eparation est tant de douleur dounce, chr'ri. Jusq'a ce que nous r'eunissons de nouveau.

### A cow boy in Paris

Vraiment, Amaury

Rawlin stuffed the note into his pocket and headed down to the lobby to get some breakfast. When he finished, he hailed the waitress.

"Could you do a little favor and read this note to me, please? I'm afraid I don't read French very well." He pulled the note from his pocket and handed it to the girl. She read it, smiling as she read it to herself, then aloud.

"Parting IS such sweet sorrow, cowboy, with you until we meet again, Cheri.

Vraiment, Amaury."

The girl grinned at Rawlin as she handed it back to him, making him blush even more since she knew the note had been written to him by a man.

"Thank you." Rawlin handed her a generous tip and left the place quickly. He stuffed the note deep into his pocket, patting it a later. He was not able to wipe the smile from his face, no matter how hard he tried. It would be a good day

## chapter 5

Again, what to do with the day? He could do anything he wanted! That was the joy of his lifestyle, was it not? The appeal, this freedom; he had no one in the world to answer to but himself.

Remembering the ride the night before, Amaury decided to stroll to the Tower Eiffel.

Amaury remembered the history he'd read of how many people thought it hideous and wanted it torn down, but they had been wrong.

Whenever he arrived, Amaury had to deal with the line of locals and tourists who had the same idea that he'd had, but it would be worth the wait. Amaury liked to walk up the first six hundred and seventy-four steps to the second level. It was refreshing. From the second platform, even though they 1,664 more steps to the top, respectively. Amaury rode the lift up to the summit for the grandest view of Paris.

At the top, he looked out over his beloved city, and his thoughts returned to Rawlin for some reason. Right about now, he would be heading for work at Rouen. Had the American had a chance to come to the top of the tower? He would have to ask him the next time he saw him. Yes, he'd decided there would be a next time.

Amaury looked in the direction of the fields beyond the city, toward his former life and home. They would be busy with the vineyards and doubted they missed him at all. He shook his head, clear of the memory. He should be doing something worthwhile today. He should sketch. Yes! He was in the mood to draw. He would have to go back to his locker for the messenger bag with his sketch pad and pencils. Amaury headed down the lift to the bottom, this time, and for the train station. As he rode, he thought of maybe finding a nice spot on the Seine, or perhaps across from one of the little Cafés where the little old ladies came for an espresso and chat, each morning, or the mother with her young infant, who would stop for an espresso. They always made for good sittings.

Amaury would end up sitting across from one of the Cafes, sketching two grey-haired women talking and laughing. He concentrated hard, working the outline with his charcoal bits. He had been there almost two hours and was beginning another sketch of the café itself and a young woman sitting alone when someone blocked the sun with their shadow. Amaury looked up, annoyed. He sprung to his feet.

"Amalie!" He threw his arms around his sister's neck and stepped back to take a look at her. "You get more beautiful each time I see you, Cheri." Kiss, kiss. Amaury pulled up a chair next to his.

"You look too thin, Amaury. Do you eat?"

"My tastes, they change of late. Things I used to like, I no longer. My appetite is strange. It changes. It's fine." That was true. For some reason, his appetite had changed, and things did not sit on his stomach so well. He'd just not eat for fear of it making him sick, sometimes, or just eat bread. Amalie patted his cheek.

"Well, I miss the rosy cheeks, brother." She looked worried. "You know I will always be here for you, don't you, darling? I love you." He looked up from his sketch, smiling but not reciprocating. I love you were words people threw around anyway, so they had lost their importance in his mind. She didn't seem to mind that he didn't answer her. She simply reached into her bag and pulled out an envelope. Amaury knew what was in it; money, as always. "Here, put this away somewhere safe." He took the envelope and put it into his bag. "Do you have food at home?"

"I am fine, Amalie. She came to find him every couple of months, bring him some money, checked on him, and see how he was doing. That is the truth."

"Where do you live these days?" Amaury smiled gestured to the area around him, to the city.

"Paris! Paris and these rails and streets are my home." He laughed, but she scowled at him, not amused.

"Seriously, Amaury, where do you keep your things, even?" The chain around his neck hung two small keys for train station lockers.

"I rent lockers in two rail stations in my city. It is the perfect storage."

"Oh, Amaury, please find a place to live. It's not safe to live on these streets. And you, of course, have to be safe in more ways than some. Are you being safe?" She'd never acknowledged that he was hustling and needed to be safe from STDs, but they both knew that's what she meant.

"Yes, I am safe in those respects, my sister, be assured."

Amaury went back to the sketch but realized that his subject had moved on.

"Amaury, I'm pregnant. I'm going to have a baby." Amaury almost dropped his sketch pad as he jumped up. Then he threw his arms around her neck again.

"Your having a baby is the most wonderful news that I have heard in a long, long time, Amalie. I'm sure Loren is elated, yes?" She smiled and began to cry with happiness. Loren was Amalie's husband.

"Yes, he is SO happy! It's a boy. Loren and I talked about it, and we need to ask your permission, but we'd like to name him Arnaud Amaury." Amaury suddenly became emotional himself and nodded. It would be very fitting to honor their brother this way.

"I think Arnaud would be most proud to have this boy named for him, as I will be. It's perfect." Amalie wiped a tear away that fell down his cheek away. They hugged and cried. "And he will be a happy boy, with no problems. Keep him away from your father and mother, and your boy will stay happy, sister."

She frowned at him. They tried to avoid the sensitive topic.

"Amaury, they're your parents too, and I can't deny them their first grandchild. Surely you can see this. They will not make him unhappy."

Amaury began to gather his things into the bag and stood up angrily.

"They deny me, Amalie, and they killed Arnaud! Yet your say they won't make him unhappy only if he's perfect will that happens. Better hope he's not gay or bi-polar, or they will make him leave, as well, or kill him!" Amalie stood up, grabbing him by the arm to keep him from going.

"You know that Arnaud killed himself, and you left home, Amaury."

Amaury's mouth hung open. Surely she knew what had happened. How could she not have? He was very angry with her, despite her news.

"Arnaud was bi-polar, and they refused to get him medication, Amalie. You must understand this. If he'd had help, he would be alive."

"Amaury, that's your opinion of the situation." He was vehemently shaking his head at her.

"No, when Arnaud was thirteen, remember, they take him to the doctors in town, then to the city?" She nodded. "He was sick. He tells me what they determined about him and that he had a chemical imbalance. They argue that he is just a moody teenager who will outgrow this. Well, he didn't, did he?"

He walked away, leaving her in the shock of this news, and then turned back. "Just pray that your baby is perfect, or his future is bleak if you stay with that family!"

He ran across the street with her, yelling after him to stop. But he just dashed down an alleyway and kept on running. Damn it! Why had he let himself get all emotional and bring back all of those memories again? It was best to forget all of them, except for Arnaud, and move on.

Walking and walking, his head began to hurt and then throb. It just got worse. Amaury decided that he'd better hide the envelope of money. It was stupid to walk around with it this way, so he headed for the train station.

When he was lonely, Amaury wished he had someone on the trains. Perhaps just someone to hold him and say that everything would be okay, or just to listen to him when he needed. But, would he ever have someone like that? It just all seemed so bleak sometimes.

Amaury unlocked the door at his locker, sticking the envelope inside one of the novels he had inside it. Then he decided to ride the rails for the rest of the day, for it was beginning to rain a bit.

## Chapter 6

It had been one hell of a day. First, the company Rawlin had been working within Rouen had run into a delay. There would be no work today after they'd wasted time sitting around. By the time his train rolled back into the Paris station, it was almost eleven o'clock.

Rawlin stepped from the train and looked around. There was no sign of Amaury at all. Damn. He was looking forward to seeing the kid again. He looked through the station and out on the street, but it just wasn't going to happen.

Rawlin hailed a cab, chastising himself again for wanting a man, let alone this guy. He was a hustler, for heaven's sake. He was probably playing the same game with half a dozen other men in the city. Let them learn to yearn for him, and then he'd get more money for his services. The boy could tell Rawlin had money. He'd told him so. He'd gotten a meal and a warm bed for the night and tired of Rawlin. "You're a fool," he muttered, drawing the attention of the driver. "I'm just talking to myself," he explained and smiled.

The taxi pulled to a stop at his hotel, and Rawlin, feeling very tired and alone, paid the man and crawled out. He closed the door and turned. As he did so, out of the corner of his eye, he saw Amaury. He was sitting on the ground in the dark corner of the building. He hugged his long legs to his chest. Rawlin thought he looked lonely.

Rawlin offered him a hand up. Amaury took it, pulling himself to his feet, relieved to see the cowboy arrive back at the hotel. Rawlin gestured toward the door, and the two of them headed that way.

Amaury was afraid to talk, still very emotional about his long day. He could feel the eyes of the staff on him as they walked through the lobby and onto the elevator. So inside, he kept his head down. He couldn't look at Rawlin and keep his composure.

When they got off the elevator, they walked to the room where Rawlin handed Amaury the card key. The door opened quickly, and they went inside.

Amaury dropped the card on the bar and his bag on the floor next to the couch, and then he just stood there, head still down.

Rawlin realized he must be upset about something. He walked behind the boy, asking him what was wrong. The words sent Amaury over the edge. He quickly turned and threw his arms around Rawlin's chest and cried. Rawlin didn't push him away. The kid's raw emotional display so moved him that he almost got teary-eyed himself.

"Come over here, and let's sit on the couch." He led the guy to the couch. Rawlin put his arm around Amaury's shoulder, and then Amaury buried his head into Rawlin's chest, still sobbing. Rawlin let him get it out of his system as he gently rubbed the boy's back as he cried. It made Amaury feel safer than he could remember, here in this man's arms. After a while, the sobbing turned to tears, and then they stopped. Amaury sat up, sniffling and wiping his face. Rawlin handed him a couple of tissues from the end table. He didn't move his arm from around the boy's shoulder, which Amaury noticed. "Sometimes, you just need to let go and let it out of you." Amaury blew his nose. "It took me over two years to let myself cry over my wife and baby. Her name was Leslie. She was so sweet."

"Two years to cry? Why so long?"

"Because I thought that men aren't supposed to break down or lose it like that. It's being a man, but that just made it worse, keeping it all in for that long." Finally, Rawlin felt Amaury's body begin to relax next to his.

"Were you glad to see me again? Honesty, please." Rawlin squeezed his shoulder.

"Yes, baby, I was glad to see you. I was so bummed when I didn't see you at the train station." Amaury smiled. He was wanted by someone, after all.

"My sister comes today. She will have a baby." The news sounded good to Rawlin.

"You're going to be an uncle, Amaury. That's great!" Amaury hadn't thought of that at all. He would be an Uncle. He was suddenly very proud of the idea.

"Yes, I will. The baby boy is to be named after my brother and me."

Now Rawlin wondered if Amaury had told him the truth about his family.

"I thought you said that you have no family. They didn't want you anymore."

"No last name. No parents. My sister, Amalie, her husband, Loren, and my papa, Henri, are still my family. She comes to find me sometimes, with news, and check on me." Rawlin was glad to hear that the Amaury had someone.

"I'm kinda relieved. I was worried about you being alone out there."

Amaury was genuinely touched that he cared.

"This baby is good news, but he has much to face. His happiness, I fear, will not be so." Rawlin was beginning to realize why this boy was so mature for his age. He'd been through a lot.

"He'll be happy sometimes, and sad, others. And whenever he's sad, he can come to his uncle to help him see it through. Family is supposed to do that, you know? Help you through the tough times." Amaury wasn't so convinced.

"But what happens if the family is the reason for sadness? What then?"

Rawlin didn't say anything, so he continued, "And what if he is like me, gay, or bi-polar, like my brother who dies?" Amaury sunk back into the sadness of the day. Rawlin hugged him with both arms now and kissed the top of his head.

"As long as he has someone to guide him and get him help if he needs it, he will be fine, I think. Always be there for him. Can you do that?"

Amaury looks up at Rawlin, kissing him gently on the lips. Rawlin didn't push him away this time, so he kissed him a second time, longer. Rawlin didn't think anymore.

So many feelings welled up inside him. He pulled Amaury into his lap and kissed him again, like a starving man. Amaury almost swooned from these kisses, and many men had kissed him, but it never felt like this. He turned his body to straddle Rawlins lap, facing him. The two of them stared into one another's eyes for a few seconds. Amaury was giving Rawlin the chance to stop, but he saw in his eyes that the cowboy didn't want him to stop. He grabbed the bottom of his shirt, and Rawlin helped him pull it over his head and threw it on the floor. Amaury reached forward and began to unbutton Rawlins shirt. They kissed, hot with passion. Amaury ground his hips against Rawlin's. The heat broke the spell for Rawlin, bringing him back to the real world and its limitations. He gently took Amaury s hands into his. Softly he told the guy he had to stop.

"I have to stop now, baby." Amaury was so disappointed. What had he done wrong this time? Rawlin could see the worry in his eyes. "It's not you, baby. It's me. I'm just…it's me, okay?" Amaury put his hands around Rawlins's neck and rocked back and forth.

"It does not feel as if you want me to stop there." Rawlin kissed him.

"Yeah," Rawlin smiled, "but up here," he pointed to his head, "tells me I need to stop. Please understand." Amaury slid off his lap, leaning against his body. Rawlin sighed. "Wow! That was not what I expected at all." Amaury lay back on the couch, giggling.

"You mean this in a good way, I hope?" Rawlin looked down at the beautiful boy and rubbed his leg.

"That's putting it mildly, honey." Amaury giggled again, happy. Rawlin got up. "I need a cold shower right now, a freezing shower." He walked out to the guy's giggles. Amaury stretched out on the couch, soaking in what had just happened between him and his cowboy. It was good.

Amaury had finished one Cosmo and made himself another, taking it into the bedroom while Rawlin was in the shower. He kicked off his shoes and socks, lying back on the bed. He propped up some pillows and turned on the stereo, sipping his drink as he waited on Rawlin to come out. Rawlin came out with a towel wrapped around him. In his haste to take a cold shower, he had neglected to grab any underwear to put on. He told this to Amaury whenever he saw that he was on the bed. Amaury gave him a suggestive look.

"You can go without them. I wouldn't mind." Rawlin grabbed a pair of silk maroon underwear. They were looser, so maybe he wouldn't be so obvious. Rawling quickly pulled them on in the closet and threw the towel into the hamper. He did not want Amaury to go, but after what had happened between them, how was he supposed to lay net to this boy and not touch him? Rawlin took a deep breath. Amaury stood up to take off his jeans while Rawlin turned down the covers. Both of them crawled into bed, and Rawlin turned off the lights. In the dark, their eyes adjusted to the darkness.

"What?" Rawlin asked of him. Amaury just smiled.

"I just like looking at you. Looking, kissing, touching, you, and…." Rawlin put a finger to Amaury's lips, silencing him.

"It's been a long day, baby, for both of us, and a lot has happened. So let's get a good night's sleep, okay?"

"Oui…….a lot has happened today. We sleep." He turned away from Rawlin, curled up, and fell asleep right away.

Rawlin watched him for a while, but soon, he, too, was asleep.

As before, Amaury rose, dressed, and was on his way to the street early in the morning before the sun came up. He left Rawlin a note again.

"Je sens en securite' ave vous.

Baisers,

Amaury"

He would take it back down to breakfast with him and hope the same waitress as before would be there. She was. He ordered crepes, and she told him that the note said,

"I feel safe with you.

Kisses, Amaury"

As he ate his breakfast, Rawlin wondered about Amaury. Was it possible that love between two men could work? He hardly knew this guy, yet he felt more emotionally connected with him than he ever had with anyone, even Leslie. It had been a comfortable, safe relationship with her that worked in his favor. Whenever Rawlin checked his messages, one from the company in Rouen wanted to renegotiate some of the project's costs. He needed to meet with their reps for a working lunch at noon.

Rawlin headed for the train station. He looked around—no Amaury. On the train, he wondered what the boy did all day. He said he sketched and hustled, and that was all. Was that what he did with his days, or was he with another man? And what was he doing right at this moment?

## Chapter 7

After a walk along the Seine, Amaury wasn't feeling so well. He had another headache, but it was because he hadn't bothered to eat at all today. So he found a café and got a pastry and some hot tea. It made him feel a bit better.

It had begun to drizzle, so he decided to make his way to the rails and one of his lockers. He would get his jacket out so that he could stay dry. But when he got there, as he could see the lockers, his heart stopped. The doors of many lockers hung open, some even torn to one hinge. Someone had broken into them. Amaury broke into a run. Not his locker, please! But as he got there, he saw that his locker was one of those. Amaury yelled out and slammed the broken door so hard that it fell to the ground. He looked inside. The jacket he'd come to get was gone. The novels he had inside were still there, so the money must be, too. He held his breath as he looked through the book he'd stored the envelope inside. It wasn't there, so he frantically checked all of them. It was gone. All of his money was gone, as well as most of his clothes. Amaury slammed his fist on the lockers. "Damn!" He hit it again, three times. "Damn! Damn! Damn!"

Amaury sank to his knees, holding his head in his hands, crying. After a few minutes, he told himself he had to get up and get a grip on himself. First, he had to assess his situation. He looked into his bag to see how much money he had there. He had two dollars. Did he have any money stored in the other locker? Yes, an American ten-dollar bill! He put the items he had left into his bag, boarded the train, and rode to the other station. Thankfully, this locker was secure. Amaury unlocked it and looked inside. He remembered that he'd already spent the American ten dollars on the way there.

He had a pair of brown jeans, two shirts, four pairs of underwear, and a red scarf in this locker. There were a few coins there but no other money. He'd just have to get to work, that's all. He put the messenger bag inside and then locked it back up. It was his fault that he'd made no money. He'd spent his time with Rawlin instead of working or sketching just for himself. Now, things would be tight. Amalie wouldn't be back for a while so he couldn't depend on her. And now that he had no money, he was hungry. He needed to save the two dollars for an emergency.

Amaury rode back to the main terminal and cruised. Unfortunately, the rain was thinning, so his prospects were minimal during this time of the day. He did manage to pick up a couple of men for quick work but not much money. And the hunger began to make him a bit nauseous.

Remembering Michael, a boy he occasionally had sex with in exchange for a free meal, was now working at Café Americana, so he headed there in the hopes of getting that meal. It was a lovely arrangement, and Amaury liked Michael and enjoyed messing around with him. Michael was always glad to see him, as he was today.

"Amaury!" He gave him a 'kiss kiss' and a huge hug. "I have not seen you in a long time. How do you know that I need you just now, darling?" He kissed Amaury on the lips drawing a frown from his manager. "Come, come." They walked over to a table in the corner, where they sat. "You don't look so good, my friend. What is up with you?" Amaury tried to force a smile.

"Someone broke into my locker and stole all of my money, Michael. I am starving. You are hungry for me?" Michael smiled, laughed, and nodded.

"I am always hungry for you, beautiful! Pick anything you wish to eat. Michael takes care of his Amaury." He kissed Amaury's cheek then handed him a menu. Amaury made his choice, Michael disappeared into the kitchen, and soon, Amaury had his meal. Now, he had to pay for it. The two boys headed for the back room to take care of business.

As Amaury walked out of the cafe, he realized that he had nowhere to go, and no one seemed to be out and about. Soon, he started to feel bad again, and the headache returned along with a stomach ache. The rain returned in a downpour. Amaury found the nearest awning to stand.

Suddenly he felt light-headed. He threw up and kept throwing up. He noticed that there was blood there, and it scared him. That had never happened before. Perhaps a clinic could give him some samples of something for his head and stomach. He had to walk in the rain and out of the way to the only clinic he knew of that he thought was open.

Amaury looked and felt terrible by the time he walked into the door of the clinic. The woman at the desk watched the TV and seemed annoyed that he had interrupted her show. "I need to see a doctor. I feel very poorly, and I threw up blood just now." She turned down the volume on the TV and handed him some forms.

"You've got to fill these out for me, first." Amaury took a pen and went to one of the chairs to sit as he filled in the information. He filled in all he wanted to share and returned the forms to the woman. She told him that he had to fill in all of the blanks. "It's required," she told him.

"That is all the information that I have to give." She seemed to understand and told him to have a seat. He didn't have to wait long. He was the only patient in the clinic. A nurse came out to lead him into the back to the doctor. He sat on the examining table to wait. By now, his head was throbbing, and his body was aching. He was so cold. He hugged himself and held his stomach as still as he could. The doctor soon appeared.

"Amaury, bonjour." The young man read over his chart. "You vomited blood? Has this happened before today?" Amaury told him that it was the first time.

"Lie down and let me see." The doctor began to squeeze his stomach. It hurt in a couple of spots. "Does this hurt?"

"It's only sore. I get a sick stomach sometimes and can't eat. And I have headaches a lot."

"I'd like to get a urine sample and take some blood. We'll test it, and you come back in two days and see what we found out, okay?" Amaury nodded.

The nurse returned to take his temperature and blood pressure. "Draw some blood, please, and get a urine sample." Amaury sat up, and the nurse gave him a cup. Amaury wanted to ask about the pills.

"Can you give me some pills for the aches and pains? I have no money."

The doctor shook his head. The clinic had been out of samples due to many requests during the past few weeks. Amaury nodded,

A cow boy in Paris

disappointed. He headed back out into the heavy rain.

## Chapter 8

Rawlin was happy with the way things had gone in Rouen. He'd put on his best 'good ole' boy' Texan personality, and things had all worked themselves out. He was reasonable, and the company knew it, but still made good for his own company. He didn't like the negotiation part of his job, but he knew he was good at it. So did George, his boss. So he'd ended the day early and boarded the train back to Paris, sleeping most of the way. The work was mentally challenging, unlike his old rough-necking days of the past, in the oilfields of Texas.

At the Paris station, he did not expect to see Amaury at all this early in the day, so he didn't even bother to look. The rain was pouring down for the trip back to his hotel, so Rawlin hurried inside toward the elevator. The manager pulled him to the side.

"Mr. Jones, there is a young man here who claims that he is an acquaintance of yours." He leaned closer to whisper, "He is not the best sort of boy, sir, if I may say so. He's been here almost an hour." The man pointed to a room across the lobby. "We moved him in here since he looks so, well, you can see for yourself." They walked over to the room, and then the manager walked away. There sat Amaury, wet to the bone, with a hotel security guard sitting next to him. He looked so small, young, and pitiful. Rawlin nodded to the guard.

"He's with me. I'll take care of it." The man nodded and left the two of them alone. Rawlin went to Amaury. "Come on. Let's get you out of those wet clothes before you get sick." He held out his hand to the boy, who took it. As they walked across the lobby, Rawlin dared anyone to say something and held his head high. He nodded at the manager, who'd been kind enough not to kick Amaury out of the hotel, then the elevator doors closed behind them. Rawlin looked at the boy. "Could you get any wetter, baby? Geez! I'm sorry they treated you that way." Amaury was used to it.

"I tell you they know I hustle. The hotel doesn't want my kind here."

Rawlin used the card key correctly on the first try at the room. "Bout fucking time," he said and laughed as they walked inside the room. "Go on and get yourself a hot shower, sweetie." They both headed into the bedroom, and Rawlin went into the closet. He yelled back at Amaury, "You got any dry clothes with you?" Amaury didn't. "Okay, just take your shower and get into bed and get warm. We'll worry about clothes later." Rawlin had to finish some paperwork, and he did so while Amaury was in the shower.

Amaury had never felt so bad. He was shivering, and his teeth chattered. He quickly got out of the wet clothes and into the hot water. Its sting felt like a message to his aching body. He let the water run over his head, then directly on his neck and shoulders for a while. It was heavenly. He stayed under the water for a long time.

Rawlin had changed into a pair of black, three-striped Adidas pants and a white t-shirt. Whenever he heard the water turn off, he headed for the bathroom with a big, soft towel. He gently began to dry Amaury's body. "That's much better." Amaury took the towel to finish his hair and the rest of his body.

"Oui is better, thank you." Rawlin playfully slapped his bare ass with his hand.

"Get that cute ass of yours into bed and snuggle up, baby." Amaury surprised himself by blushing a little bit. He smiled and then headed for the bed, getting under the covers. "You want an extra blanket? There's more in the closet." Amaury nodded, so Rawlin got one and threw it across the bed. Though he'd pulled the covers up to this neck, he was still cold, and his teeth chattered a little. Rawlin figured it was because of his wet hair. He would be warm soon.

"Hey, I'm going to have your clothes sent out to room service. Is that okay?"

"Oui," Amaury whispered. Rawlin walked over to sit on the edge of the bed.

"You realize that this means that you'll have to be here whenever I wake up? I know you have your rules, so I just wanted to make sure you understood."

Amaury had always stuck to his rules, yes, but now, here with Rawlin, something was different. Something had changed. Rawlin wanted him there in the morning.

"Send them to the launders." Rawlin nodded and then leaned over, kissing him. He gathered Amaury's wet clothes and some of his dirty ones, put them in the laundry bag, and set them out in the hallway. He then went back to Amaury's side. "I'm going to order some soup and crackers from room service to warm you up. You need to eat something. I'll bet you haven't."

"This is what upsets me. I did eat, and then I get sick." Rawlin still insisted that soup and crackers would be good for him.

"It's the perfect thing for you. It will warm you up from the inside out, and with some club soda, will settle your stomach."

Rawlin walked out to the parlor to ring room service, and then he went back into the bedroom. "I'm going to take a quick shower before our food arrives. You just take care of yourself and rest." Amaury nodded and closed his eyes, a smile on his face.

Amaury must have nodded off as soon as Rawlin turned the water on, for whenever he woke, it was almost nine o'clock. Rawlin sat near the bed in a rocking chair, reading. He wore a pair of black-framed reading glasses. Amaury thought he looked younger in them and very sexy. He had put on red plaid pajama pants with a tight ribbed tank top. His cowboy was a hunk!

"What are you reading?"

Rawlin jumped, startled by the sound of Amaury's voice breaking the silence. He pulled off his glasses and put the book down.

"You're awake." He moved to sit on the bed and then put the back of his hand to Amaury's face. "No fever. That's good." Rawlin patted his cheek. He remembered the question. "The Haunted Mesa." Amaury looked at him.

"You asked me what I was reading. That's what it's called. It's a Louis L'amour book. It's excellent."

"May I read when you finish?" Rawlin liked the idea of them sharing a book for some corny reason.

"Sure you can. I've already read it a dozen times. It's that good, to me."

Rawlin got some extra pillows from the closet. "Sit up a minute." He put the pillows behind Amaury's back. "Okay, lie back now." Amaury did, carefully. "Are you hungry? I just need to warm it up for you, and that will only take a minute."

"Oui, very hungry." Rawlin was up and out of the room before he could say another word. In the kitchenette, he popped the soup container into the microwave. When it's warm, Rawlin placed it on a breakfast tray he'd found, along with a spoon, crackers, melon pieces, and a glass of Seven-up, with ice in it. When he carried it into the bedroom, Amaury looked so sweet, sitting up in bed, the covers neatly turned to his waist. Rawlin carefully sat the tray down and laid a napkin onto Amaury's chest. Amaury felt special, which made him a little melancholy. No one ever did anything like this for him since he was young. "Thank you for taking care of me." Rawlin smiled.

"You're welcome, but you don't worry about anything. Just eat something and build your strength. Don't overeat, or it could make you sick again."

Rawlin sat down in the rocker again.

"Sorry, but I've already eaten. It smelt so good, and I couldn't wait for you.

It's delicious." Amaury ate slowly. Rawlin was right. It might make him sick again.

Rawlin talked about his day and how well things had gone as he ate.

"I got a good deal out of them. And all the while, the company thinks we're making a big sacrifice for them, but it's just fair business. We want their business again." Amaury ate half of the soup, put down his spoon, and smiled at Rawlin. It was a different smile and one Rawlin hadn't seen before. The guy's eyes were happy. "What? Do you need something else?" Amaury shook his head.

"No, I have what I need right here." The statement flew right over Rawlins's head at first, and then he got it, blushing. Amaury finished eating.

"Let me just get that out of your way." Rawlin took the tray back into the kitchen and then returned. Amaury was just about to ask him what his job was whenever Rawlins cell phone rang. He looked to see who it was. It was his boss, George. "Gotta take this, honey." He stepped into the next room. "George, what's going on?"

"We had a great day today." George Arkin had been a great boss. He trusted Rawlin to make good decisions and wasn't hovering around or second-guessing him all the time.

"Yes, I heard, Rawlin. That's one of the reasons that I'm calling. That was one hell of a deal you got us. Good work! Course, I should have expected that from you." Rawlin knew it was good, but sometimes he still needed to hear it.

"Thanks. It worked out that way. They're good people. I like working with'em." Rawlin sat on the couch.

"What the hell are you doing staying in Paris instead of Rouen? That train ride must get old." Rawlin laughed.

"Yeah, but Paris is Paris, George. I have a little downtime, and there's so much to do here in the city." George said that he was surprised. He didn't see Rawlin as the Paris type. Rawlin just laughed.

"The other reason I called is that your Dad called me. He said he didn't have your cell number, just the business one. That true, Rawlin?" Rawlin knew it sounded terrible, but he wanted it that way. He could talk to who he wanted to but not to whom he didn't.

"Yeah, that's true. Let's keep it that way, George? Do me that favor." His boss agreed that he would, though he didn't think it was a good idea, the way Rawlin isolated himself from family. "It just works for me, George."

George and Kenny Jones had worked together in the old days. They were still friends. "Was something wrong?" They never called unless something was.

"They want you to come home for the holidays, Rawlin. This year, they want the whole family back at the farm in Abernathy. They moved back there."

"They did? What the hell for?" The farm was where he'd grown up, but his parents had bought a spread outside Lubbock not far from his place whenever he was a junior at Texas Tech.

"Some guy gave them $50,000 over what their place was worth. He just stopped by and made an offer. Gonna run a horse boarding place there. That long ago? Course, he hadn't spoken with them in a long, long time. So your parents sold and moved back to the farm in June."

"So, they want me to come home." The thought made Rawlins's stomach tighten. "Did you tell them that I've got this Paris job coming up after the Rouen one?" George said that it looked like the Paris job would be put off for a while, and a job in Montreal would be next for Rawlin. "Montreal?"

"Yep, Montreal is coming up between now and Christmas, so, since you're going to be in America anyway, I told them that you could come by the farm."

Rawlins heart nearly leaps from his chest. He stood up. Now, what would he do?"

"George, why the hell would you tell them that? What if I don't want to see them for my reasons?" He was getting angry with George.

"Rawlin, you've been gone a long, long time, and you never dealt with Leslie's death. Maybe it's time to do that by reconnecting with your family."

"Well, we'll see. I'm going to let you go, George. I've got company right now."

Why had he said that? He never talked about anything personal with George.

"Oh, I get it. You've met someone in Paris, haven't you? You dog! Just take her home for Christmas. They'll be thrilled that you've met someone." Rawlins's eyes got big. Yeah, he could just see that if he took a dude home with him.

"I'll talk to ya later, George." He hung up. Rawlin sighed heavily. He just wouldn't even think about leaving Paris right now, let alone going home for Christmas. He headed back into the bedroom. "That was my boss. He heard about the deal I got us today. He's happy. That's good." Amaury's eyes were heavy. "I see you're tired, too. I'm looking forward to waking up with you, for once. Let's get some sleep."

Rawlin turned down the covers, got into bed, turned off the lights, and laid down. Amaury expected Rawlin to roll over and go to sleep. Instead, he moved a little closer to Amaury, patting his chest. "Lay your head right here." Amaury rolled onto his side and laid his head on Rawlins's chest. Rawlin put his arm across his back. "Sweet dreams, baby." Amaury snuggled closer and closed his eyes to sleep.

Amaury slept well, waking once with a headache. He found some Tylenol in Rawlins shaving kit, took two, and then went back to sleep, curling into the curves of Rawlins body.

For Rawlin, it was hard to sleep at first. He woke once when the Amaury went into the bathroom. This time he felt an immense affection for Amaury that was hard to explain. Rawlin heard him digging around his things, but Rawlin trusted him. Then he listened to the pill bottle of painkillers.

When Amaury had returned to bed, Rawlin kissed him, and then they both fell back asleep.

Rawlin woke first, and it felt good to have Amaury's warm body next to him. He looked angelic in his sleep. He was lying on his stomach, the pillows and covers pushed away from his naked body. Amaury's breathing was even, and his long hair was hanging down into his face. Rawlin had to touch him, so he ran a hand alongside the young man's cheek. It was intimate yet straightforward. Amaury opened his eyes. "Good morning, beautiful."

"Good morning. Is late? I feel I slept a year." Rawlin looked over at the clock.

"Not bad, considering. It's only a little after eleven." Amaury groaned, stretched, and then got up. He marched his naked self to the bathroom to pee. As he took care of business, he called back to Rawlin.

"May I use your toothpaste?" Rawlin said that he could and an extra toothbrush in the medicine cabinet. Amaury found it, brushed his teeth, washed his face, and combed his hair before walking, slightly effeminately, back into the room, lying on the bed.

"You sure look a lot better than you did when I saw you yesterday. You feeling okay?" Amaury shrugged.

"I suppose." He shrugged again. "I'm dry, warm, and no aches now, so this is good." Rawlin was so glad he hadn't stayed out in the rain.

"It rained on and off all night long, I think. You might have caught pneumonia or something if you'd stayed out."

Rawlin needed to know something, even if he didn't like the answer. "So, are you glad you stayed to wake up with me?" Amaury thought about what to say, but he asked a question instead.

"Are you glad?" Rawlin answered by leaning his way, kissing him. "I suppose this is a yes?" Rawlin smiled and kissed him again.

"Yes, Amaury, I am glad you stayed. Is this the first time you've ever done it?"

"Oui, I've never stayed before to wake with a man. I like to control when I come and go, you understand?" Then he looked a bit sad. "And no one ever asked before. It was nice with you." Rawlin was very curious about his highly sexual being and his life.

"Have you ever been with a woman?" Amaury scowled and then grimaced.

"Non, non, not me! It won't ever happen unless by force." He giggled. "Is true that they are beautiful to look at, sketch, and dress, but is not for my pleasure in sex or intimacy, non." A knock at the door interrupted the personal conversation. Damn it! Rawlin was getting him to open up a little. He went to answer the door. When he opened it, the laundered clothes had arrived. He carried the clothes into the bedroom.

" You can get dressed now." Rawlin laid the folded laundry on the bed, and Amaury began to dress. Rawlin walked into the closet and pulled out a pair of jeans and a red button shirt. He pulled on the jeans, leaving the shirt unbuttoned. Rawlin found his brown western belt, pulling it through the loops. Whenever he turned back to the bed, Amaury was gone. "Damn it, Amaury. You didn't take off on me again, did you?" He hurried into the other room, and there he was, a big smile on his face, making coffee.

"I am no morning person, my cowboy. I need caffeine. It wakes me."

Rawlin sat down at a barstool. He needed to bring up a sensitive subject. He hadn't known how to do it, so he just said it.

"Honey, I don't know how you want me to, well, you know, take care of you." Amaury sat a cup of coffee in front of him. He didn't understand, so Rawlin tried again.

"I mean, your services, how do I take care of that?" Amaury smiled a tender smile at him.

"Cheri, to be with you is not to work." He sat on a stool next to Rawlin.

"But if you are with me, then you can't be working. Let me at least give you something to make up for that time." He pulled his wallet from his pocket and tried to give Amaury some money. Amaury pushed his hand away and continued to sip his coffee. Rawlin let it go. He just looked so adorable in his tattered jeans, barefoot, and wearing a t-shirt that was two sizes too small for him. It was purple with a magenta peace sign and a pair of lips. It was then that Rawlin noticed that his toenails were painted black. He bumped Amaury's shoulder. "Nice toes." Amaury looked down at his feet, raising one to show Rawlin.

"You like them? A man I see had a foot fetish. He turns on to paint them." Amaury laughed, and Rawlin shook his head.

"Honey, if I showed up with painted toenails like that, back in Texas, they'd kick my ass or worse!" Amaury thought he was kidding at first, and then he was shocked.

"Serious? For painted nails, they hurt you in Texas? This is scary."

"It's not a cowboy kinda thing to do." Amaury got a sugar cube for himself and one for Rawlin. He plopped them into the cups. They sat there, drinking coffee, not needing to talk every second. Finally, Rawlin spoke. "Looks like it's going to be a lovely day. Let's finish this coffee out on the balcony." With a nod from Amaury, they headed out to sit in the chairs there.

"If you'll spend the day with me, I'll take the day off. You can show me around this city you love so much." Amaury looked out at the view, thinking. He couldn't give too much. In his three years on the streets, he'd had offers to be kept by a few men, and it would be easy to say 'yes,' but he never had. He would lose his freedom. But what exactly was that? Loneliness and no one who was waiting for him?

Rawlin was getting worried by the look on Amaury's face and the lack of an answer. "Just for the day, honey. I want to spend it with you if you'd like to."

Amaury had a question for him, first.

"Why do you want to be with me, anyway?" It was a legitimate question but not easily put into words by Rawlin. He hoped he didn't fumble things up.

"Amaury, I never just take a day off for fun, not ever, okay? And now I want to, and I chose to do it with you." The answer seemed to satisfy Amaury. He smiled and nodded.

"Only for you, Cheri." He kissed Rawlin on the cheek. Rawlin was so excited that he was like a little boy getting candy or something. He jumped up.

"Just let me make a couple of calls first, and then we can decide where we want to get started." Rawlin headed inside to make the calls. While he was gone, Amaury thought about this. He had to let Rawlin know he was his person. He made a decision. If Rawlin got the day, then he'd lose the night. It was a compromise that Rawlin had to deal with. He told Rawlin, who carried the phone closer to the balcony. Rawlin put his hand over the phone. Rawlin was disappointed.

"But why? Why don't you want to stay the whole night and day, giving me twenty-four hours with you?" But Amaury was firm.

"Because I am my boss, owned by no one, cowboy." He stared Rawlin down. Rawlin started to respond, but he had to finish his call.

"Yes, hello, Marie, it's Rawlin Jones. I'm just letting you know that I'm taking the day off today. If anything comes up, just leave a message with the hotel. I won't have my phone with me." Amaury watched and listened. "Yeah, you can just fax those plans over to Sebastian for me. That would be great, Marie."

Amaury carried his coffee back into the kitchen, pouring it down the drain. He rinsed out the cup and then the sink. He put it back into the cupboard while Rawlin made another call. Then they got ready.

"My shoes, Rawlin?" Rawlin pointed toward the bedroom, so he went in and found them on the far side of the bed. Amaury sat down to slip the clean socks on and then his brown loafers. Rawlin came in and sat next to him on the bed, playfully bumping his shoulder with his own.

"Listen, Amaury. It's not like I go around doing this in every city I work. It's the first time I've ever done it, and I'm not asking you to make any commitment to me." Amaury put a finger to Rawlins's lips. He knew this was all new to the American and found it cute to have him explain.

"I know my cowboy." Rawlin nodded and kissed him. Then, just to lighten the heavy mood, he put Amaury into a headlock and messed with his hair. Amaury yelled, giggled, and tried to break free. He bit Rawlins's arm, so he let go. "Ah, you ask for trouble, Jones. Watch yourself!" Rawlin hugged him. "Now, what do you wish to do in my romantic city?" He gestured the world.

Rawlin got up to get his boots and socks, put them on, and then sat again.

"I'm going to let you decide where to take me. I'll like it as long as you take me there." Rawlin began to button his shirt, but Amaury ran a hand over his chest, stopping him.

"Leave it open a minute, cowboy." He ran his hand across Rawlin's chest again and then leaned down, kissing one then the other of his nipples, biting them lightly. It was very erotic, and Rawlin was quickly hard. He groaned and then took Amaury by the shoulders, holding him back.

"Later, baby," he said in a suggestive tone. Rawlin stood up to button the shirt and then tucked it in. Amaury gave him an up and down, then Rawlin got his watch and wallet and then clapped his hands together. "Well, let's get going!"

They headed down to the lobby, not caring about the looks they got from anyone along the way.

They were both hungry, so Amaury took Rawlin to a café called 'Le Select,' where they ordered tartines (slices of buttered bread with fruit topping). It was good, and they had fun watching the people passing by, guessing who they were and where they were going. Before they left, Amaury asked what he'd already done in Paris.

"This time, I've done nothing but work, honey. I'm not pretty enough to do what you do." Amaury playfully stuck out his tongue out at Rawlin, and they laughed.

"These awful American tourists with we must deal. Tsk, tsk. They only want their McDonald's to eat and be with other Americans." Amaury shook his head, walking backward to Rawlin. "Shall we avoid with the rude French?" He liked teasing the man.

"No, smartass, that's okay, and hey, we aren't all like that, just like you guys aren't all rude." He swiped at Amaury, who managed to get out of his way quickly.

"Do I slow for you, old man?" Rawlin chastised him for the remark anAmaury came back next to him, hooking his arm in Rawlins. They walked a few more feet, and then Amaury asked him, "Just how old are you anyway?" Rawlin knew this would have to come up one of these days. He grinned a little.

"If I tell you the truth, you aren't gonna run away as fast as you can, are you?" Amaury laughed, shaking his head. Rawlin loved to hear him laugh.

"I'm twenty-eight years old, kid." Rawlin held his breath, waiting for Amaury's response. Amaury hadn't been far off with his guess.

"You are not old, Rawlin, as I am not a kid, despite my years. Besides, it's a number, nothing more." Rawlin was so relieved that he hadn't been rejected because of the age difference. He did feel like a cradle robber sometimes.

"I have plans, now. We are going to Notre Dame! Come on, cowboy." He pulled Rawlin along.

"I'm coming. I'm coming." Hey, where can we get a burner phone? I'd like to take some photos of stuff and you." Amaury wasn't thrilled about the idea, but what could he say?

"I know a place. Is pharmacy to have them." Amaury took him by the pharmacy, where Rawlin tried to buy two phones. One for Amaury, but he refused it.

"I don't want or need a mobile phone, Rawlin. Do you wish to track me, now?" Rawlin bought only one and continued the conversation outside the pharmacy.

"No, it's not for controlling you, Amaury. It's so that you can take some photos for yourself. Although it would be nice to be able to call and talk to you or ask you to meet up with me sometime." Amaury was shaking his head. Rawlin let it go.

They caught the train that would take them to the cathedral. It was only a short ride, and as the two walked up to the famous church, Rawlin was amazed by its beauty. He snapped a couple of photos.

"These pictures aren't going to do this place any justice, cowboy. It's so glorious!" Amaury hurried ahead, trying not to be in the photos, but Rawlin caught up to him. Rawlin paid for the two of them to enter the place.

"You think out here is beautiful. Just see the inside. Is stunning work!"

He took Rawlins's hand as they walked. Rawlin was worried and tried to pull away. "No, don't be afraid. It is common to see men holding hands in Paris. It is acceptable." Rawlin relaxed and felt a little bit better. He felt like a gushing teenager! He hoped the guy was telling him the truth.

Amaury walked up toward the front. Inside, hushed voices and wide eyes marveled at the architecture and art of the building. It was truly spiritual. Rawlin called out his name, causing him to turn, taking a photo.

"Stop it, Rawlin. I don't want to be in the photos." He walked with his hand on the side of his face. Rawlin didn't understand why he would care. Why didn't he say something whenever he'd bought the phone? Maybe he was just playing around with him.

Rawlin walked toward Amaury. An older American lady asked him if he wanted a photo with his son. With his son? Oh, god! He looked up to the front of the church. What was God thinking of him? He just knew how he felt about Amaury, and he wanted to have this day with him.

"Amaury, come here a minute, will you?" Amaury was still pouting, but he walked over. Rawlin had handed the phone to the woman. He put his arm around Amaury, and she snapped a photo before he could turn away. "Thank you." He took back the phone, turned around, and Amaury was gone. He was heading out the door. Damn it!

Amaury had to get out of there. He was suddenly very emotional and not quite sure why. He sat on a bench, head in his hands. That's where Rawlin found him and sat next to him. "What's wrong?" Amaury couldn't look at him just now, so he just shrugged. He wouldn't tell the man that he wanted no reminders of their time together. Soon, this cowboy would move on, and that would leave him to himself again. It would hurt too much to be reminded of their time together with a photo. He took a deep breath, got up, and looked around.

"Come on. Next stop is Musee' de Louve. We go by Metro." He pulled Rawlin and his feet, and they walked to the station that would take them to the Louvre.

On the train, Amaury leaned back, shutting his eyes, glad that Rawlin hadn't pressed him for an explanation for his behavior. Rawlin had realized that the boy needed his space and didn't want to give too much of himself away. Sometimes he was just moody. He was just so afraid to get close or attached to anyone. Rawlin could understand. He felt the same way, especially to anyone of the same sex as himself.

They departed the metro and walked to the Louvre's main entrance. Rawlin paid to get them in, and he was glad to see that Amaury's mood improved.

"To see the Louvre properly, we'd need much time. Today we do the walk-through. Which to see first, Cheri?" Rawlin wanted to see the Mona Lisa. "Excellent choice!" He led Rawlin in the direction of the famous portrait, and soon, he was laughing and having a good time again. They would end up spending almost three hours in the museum before getting too hungry. Amaury suggested a place right near there, so that's where they went.

It was a popular place due to its proximity to the Louvre. They found a seat by the window where they returned to their game of guessing who people were, what their story was, and where they were going. They talked about what they had seen so far, too. Amaury remarked that he liked the glass addition to the Louvre but felt it didn't belong there. "Is not the correct style. Is belonging somewhere else." Rawlin looked at the glass structure. He hadn't thought about it.

"I don't know. I think it looks kind of cool here. It's trendy." He took a bite of the sandwich that he'd chosen. It was pretty good.

His comment amused Amaury. It seemed something he would say instead of the older Texan. He continued to study the whole scene as they ate while Rawlin watched him. When he looked up, Rawlin was smiling at him.

"What is amusing you?" Rawlin put down his sandwich.

"You're amazing, that's all. I mean, the more time I spend with you, the harder it is to believe that you are only nineteen years old." Amaury got mad.

"I told the truth!" He was defensive and frowning. Rawlin reached across to put his hand on Amaury's arm.

"No, honey. I mean that you are very mature for your age." That melancholy look came across the boy's face again.

"I am not nineteen in my mind, Rawlin Jones." He sipped on his drink, thinking. "I've been on my own since sixteen like most French young people, but It's only me. Depending on myself for everything makes you grow fast, here." He tapped his head, "And here." He tapped his heart.

"You know, the European boys that I've met all seem so much more mature than American boys the same age. I mean, that's the way I see it." He took another bite of his sandwich.

"That's for sure. Yanks are spoiled." Rawlin laughed and coughed, choking on his drink a little.

"You got that right. Most American kids think the world owes them something simply because they were born," Rawlin told him.

"And we here do not do so. We are determined by aptitude what we do early in life. Not American Dream that you have there. Do what you desire, you know? Not here. You test, you don't do well, and you can't do that job. It's life."

Rawlin had him opening up again. He pressed for more information.

"Did you finish school before you ran away from home?" Amaury put down his sandwich, looking at Rawlin. "What?" Amaury was getting mad.

"I did NOT run away! I was thrown away! I was not this spoiled child who didn't get his way and ran to the city." Amaury started to bite his sandwich but was too mad to eat. He threw it at Rawlin instead. "I no longer am hungry!" He stood up as Rawlin grabbed a handful of napkins to clean up.

"Amaury, you have got to stop taking everything so personally. It was just a mix-up of words, and you're having a temper tantrum, throwing food at me. Sit down."

"To be thrown away and not wanted is not just…..it is no mix-up and not my temper! It is personal. My whole life is serious!" Amaury left in a huff. Rawlin continued to eat.

Amaury walked across the courtyard, pacing back and forth there. He grew more annoyed when Rawlin didn't come running out after him. He saw a girl nearby checking him out. She was smoking, so he walked over to her.

"Salute

"Salute. Cigarette?" She nodded and handed him the box. He took one out, and he lit his cigarette from hers. "Merci." He puffed on the smoke and paced a bit more, looking back toward the café now and again, frowning.

The girl began to flirt with him, saying her name was Darcy. She batted her lashes at him, and he said, "I'm Amaury, and I will save you some time. I prefer boys, Cheri." He smiled and shrugged at her. She just giggled and went her own way. "Merci, again, for the cigarette," he yelled after her.

Inside the café, Rawlin finished all he wanted to eat as he watched the scene with the girl. He then cleared the table since Amaury had made such a mess, then he leisurely strolled over to where Amaury, almost finished with his smoke, had taken a seat. Rawlin patted his stomach and stretched.

"That was pretty darned good if I do say so." He sat down. "Where to next, sweetheart?" He leaned on the boy, smiling at him.

How could one stay mad at this man? Amaury took one last drag on the cigarette and then snuffed it out on the ground. He stood up, as did Rawlin.

"We go now to the Arch de Triumph de la Carrousel." Rawlin agreed, and they began to walk again. As they walked, Rawlin surprised him by taking his hand. Amaury broke into a big smile. He walked taller and prouder.

On the Chan de Salas, they took photos up the street, with the arch in the background. Amaury didn't even complain when Rawlin took his picture this time. He even took some for Rawlin too.

As they walked closer, Amaury spoke of Arch's history, and they took more photos and then went inside the place before departing.

"Now, we go to the ultimate spot. The Tower Eiffel! Remember we saw it the first time we got together? It is one of my favorite places to be. Still, I think? It's romantic up there." Rawlin put an arm around Amaury's shoulder as they walked.

"You can't do Paris without the Eiffel Tower, can you?"

Amaury told him of his last trip to the top as they walked.

"I was there not long ago. I walk up the first two platforms and then ride to the top. It was magic!" They headed for the train. As they rode, Rawlin asked him the question that he'd been dying to ask all day.

"So what do you do all day on your own? I mean, when you aren't working?" Rawlin put his arm around the boy, pulling him close.

"Anything I want. It's very liberating, you see? I am free."

"Do you have friends your age, or anyone, to hang out with and do stuff nineteen-year-olds do?" Amaury chose to ignore the question.

"When I was walking up the tower, I think of you, Rawlin." Rawlin was surprised.

"Why would you be thinking of me when you have the world in your hands?" He hoped that didn't sound too condescending. Perhaps the boy was just making the story up.

"I think that I'd like to share the experience with you because you never have it. Now I can do this today."

"Honey, you could have anyone you want, the way you look. I know why you said you picked me in the first place, but why do you keep coming back?"

Amaury just kissed him. Again, he chose to ignore the question.

As they rode, Rawlin thought of something. "You don't expect me to walk up that thing, do you, in these boots?" Amaury smiled and nodded. Rawlin growled.

"Is only 674 steps, cowboy. The Jules Verne is there. We can get a drink."

"Now, I might just make it if we can have a drink when we get there."

As they walked to the base of the tower, it seemed more prominent than he'd remembered. Rawlin snapped some photos, including one of Amaury from behind, when he didn't realize it.

They walked up the stairs to platform one. Rawlin was a little out of breath when he got there. He tried not to show it, but Amaury would run up a few steps and then wait for him to catch up. He just grinned at Rawlin, not saying anything. They walked to the rail together, leaning shoulders as they looked out on the city. The view was incredible. Amaury laid his head on Rawlin's shoulder. It was romantic and sweet at the same time. "This is an amazing view. No wonder it's of your favorite places to visit." Amaury shook his head.

"Is one of my favorite places to go. I think the rails are my favorite." Rawlin started to ask why, and then he remembered what had happened to Arnaud.

The restaurant was here, so they went inside for the drink that Amaury said they would have. They found a table for two, and they both ordered a Cosmo.

"I'm gonna find the men's room. Be right back."

Rawlin made his way across the room. He wasn't going to the men's room. He asked one of the waiters to take a few photos of Amaury and himself without Amaury being aware. Rawlin told him that he'd get the phone on the way down. He gave the waiter a nice tip, so the young man was glad to help.

Rawlin headed back to the table just as their drinks arrived. "A toast!" Rawlin held up his glass. Amaury was a little worried about what Rawlin would say, but he breathed a sigh of relief whenever Rawlin toasted the city.

"To Paris and all of her beauty." The glasses clinked, and Amaury beamed. He knew that Rawlin meant him, as well as the city.

"To Paris!" They finished their drinks and then headed for the elevator to take them to the top. Whenever they got there, Rawlin was speechless. It was more than beautiful. It was spectacular! The lights below and the city below them all look surreal. "Take a photo of me with the city over my shoulder, honey."

He reached into his pocket. "Oh, great. I must have left my phone in the men's room." Rawlin asked a woman nearby to take a couple of photos of him. He gave her his phone number to text them later. Amaury allowed a picture of himself taken. He refused to let the woman take one of the two of them together.

"No, cowboy. The top of the Tower is a special place for lovers. Some propose matrimony up here, you know? It is sacred, of sorts." Rawlin let it go and then took Amaury's hand in his.

"Amaury, this has been the best time I've had in a long time. Thank you for sharing your city with me." Rawlin took Amaury by the hand, kissing him. Amaury met his eyes, and they began to tear up. No! He would not cry. He pulled free, whispering something.

"Je vowon pris," then he stood. "Can we go now?" They headed for the elevator. On the ride down, Amaury made it a point to stand a couple of feet away from Rawlin. They made a quick stop so that Rawlin could get his phone and then headed back down.

Rawlin didn't want the day to end when they reached the bottom. He asked Amaury where they would go next. Amaury wouldn't look at him.

"Our day is finished. I have an appointment that I must keep. I never break an appointment."

"But there's something I'd like to do for you if you'll let me." Amaury looked at him. His interest peaked. "You seem to need some clothes, baby. I'd like to buy you some." Amaury looked down at his clothes. He knew how they must seem.

"You are embarrassed by my appearance?" Rawlin shook his head.

"No, I'd just like to help you out, and I love to shop for clothes." Amaury tried to hide a smile. He would never have thought his cowboy would like to shop for clothes.

"My clothes got stolen when my locker got robbed. They took clothes, including my jacket. I have little left to wear." So that was where he kept his things. Rawlin was right. He was homeless.

"So, will you let me do this for you?" Rawlin wanted to do this.

"Only if it is a loan to repay you. Is the only way I allow you to do this."

"Okay, but you have a whole year to pay me back." Amaury had a small glimmer of hope that this meant they would still see one another in a year.

"Is deal." He offered his hand, which Rawlin shook, and then hugged Amaury.

## A cow boy in Paris

"So, where do we go to a shop? I have no idea where the cool stuff is."

Amaury thought it was adorable whenever Rawlin spoke as a young person.

Amaury knew just where to go. His favorite store was called Tati. He had stolen from them many times before, in the old days.

"Is department store is called Tati. It has clothes of youth, modern, as I like."

"It sounds good to me. Let's go!"

The two men headed for the metro rail that would take them close to the store.

Amaury and Rawlin headed into the men's department when they got there.

Amaury wasn't quite sure what was supposed to happen, and so he just stood there. "So, go look around and pick out a few things. Like jeans, shirts, a jacket, undies, and socks, you know. Just stuff you need."

Amaury began to look around the store, picking out a couple of pairs of jeans shirts, and then found Rawlin, who was looking at belts. "Sorry, no Western belts here."

Amaury liked Rawlins's attempts at humor. He was funny, not being funny.

"I go try on now. Where will you be?" Rawlin wanted to see how he looked in the clothes.

"I want you to model for me. It'll be fun, and I get to see your style." Amaury grumbled as Rawlin followed him to the dressing room. There were a couple of chairs just outside the rooms, so Rawlin had a seat there to wait for Amaury to come out as he tried on the clothes. He didn't come out, so Rawlin called him at the door. "Let me see what you look like, baby."

"I am not coming out, cowboy. I look ugly." Rawlin laughed.

"If you're not coming out here, then I'm coming back there. Make your choice. I want to see what you picked out." Amaury knew he'd do it, too. So he hung the first pair of jeans back on the hanger. They had looked silly. He pulled on the second pair. They were dark, low-rise, skinny jeans. They looked pretty good. He pulled on a lime green and yellow-striped shirt with 'Oui!' written red. He reluctantly walked out to where Rawlin sat and wolf-whistled at Amaury, who crossed his arms, blushing, even though he secretly liked it.

"God, you look good in that. Turn around and let me see that cute ass of yours." Another young boy passed by, hearing what Rawlin said. Now it was his turn to blush. The boy winked at Amaury, who smiled at him and Rawlin.

He turned around and back again. "You should defiantly get that outfit." Amaury felt silly modeling like this. He headed back into the dressing room, put on his old clothes, and came out again. He handed the shirt and jeans to Rawlin.

"I must go, Rawlin." He knelt to tie his worn shoe. Rawlin couldn't believe this guy. He was being thrifty!

"You don't have any clothes, Amaury. Get yourself at least one more outfit while I look for a jacket, okay? Then it's undies and socks, and then you can go."

Amaury sighed and looked through the clothes again while Rawlin looked at the jackets. He found a medium-weight, nylon jacket, with patches on the back with the names of famous cities worldwide, like 'Hollywood' and 'London.' It looked like it would fit, so Rawlin headed back to find Amaury. He was standing at the door of the dressing rooms, waiting for Rawlin. "Ah, there you are. Damn!" Amaury was now wearing a maroon, ribbed shirt with a pair of dark gray pants. They looked very sexy, and he told Amaury so. "You are getting that, period. And here, try this on, if you like it." He handed the jacket to Amaury, who slipped it on. He turned to look in the mirror. "Hey, it has a hood zipped up in this collar. That's perfect for when it rains. You can stay dry."

"I like it. It feels soft on the inside." Rawlin told him to get dressed and bring the clothes up to the counter. He headed for the belts again. There weren't any Western belts, but there was a black belt as close to Western as he could get in this store. He got one that looked like it would fit Amaury's tiny waist and headed for the front of the store. Amaury was there waiting for him with the two outfits in his arms. "Here, this is perfect for both of those outfits. It's not Western, but the buckle is kinda like it."

Rawlin laid the clothes on the counter and then pulled out his wallet. "Oh, damn. I must have dropped my credit card back there by the belts. Would you go get it and grab some undies and socks while you're back there, okay?"

Amaury did as asked, and Rawlin turned to the cashier. "Could you ring these up right quick, and whenever the total comes up, just say it's about half of the amount that it is?" The girl looked at him. "Please. He won't want me to spend this much on him. He deserves this stuff." The girl smiled and nodded. She'd do it. Amaury came back with the undies and socks.

"I couldn't find it, Cheri." Rawlin held up the card.

"I forgot that I put it in my pocket while we were getting drinks. Lay that stuff on here so that this young lady can ring them up." Amaury laid the things on the counter and waited for the total. He hoped it wasn't too much. He didn't want to owe Rawlin much money. He would not take a year to pay him back, no matter what. He'd pay him back as soon as possible.

"That will be $74.68 U.S. dollars ." Rawlin handed her the card, and then she rang it up. Amaury looked at the items, then back at the girl. That couldn't be right. Rawlin could see that he was suspicious, so he quickly said that the clothes were an additional 50% off. Amaury seemed to buy this.

The girl bagged up the items, and the two of them headed back out onto the street.

"I must go now, cowboy. Can you do a favor for me, please?"

"Anything, sweetie. What is it?" Amaury held the bags out to him.

"Could you keep these things for now? I can't take them to the appointment with me. I will get them later from you?" Rawlin took the bags. It made him happy to have an excuse to see Amaury again. Each time he saw him, Rawlin wondered if it would be the last.

"Sure. I'll keep the clothes for you, but when will I see you again?" Amaury took off in a jog, but he turned back to Rawlin.

"You will see me around, as before, Cheri!" He ran toward the metro.

Back to the hotel, Rawlin checked his messages at the desk. He had one from George. It said to call him no matter how late. So, up in his room, Rawlin made the call. "Hi, George, what's going on?"

"Did you check your e-mail today?" Rawlin logged on and opened his e-mail. He saw the one George was referring to, reading it.

"Rawlin, you still there? Did you get your itinerary?"

Rawlin had never confronted George like he was about to, but he had no choice.

The itinerary was for a one-way ticket to Montreal, leaving three days later.

" George, I'm not leaving Paris right now. I can't."

George didn't say anything, just sighed.

"Alright, Rawlin. I can delay the job for a while, but you are the only one who has enough experience to do this job. I need you."

"I understand. I just need a little more time here." George agreed that he could give

J. M Palmer

Rawlin a week or two, but he'd have to fly to Montreal after that.

Rawlin hung up, wondering what the hell he was going to do now. A week or two?

## Chapter 9

Amaury had put off going to the clinic. He still had headaches and got sick to his stomach. The doctor sent him to a nearby hospital outpatient center for an upper GI and an MRI. It was kind of scary going through this alone. Amaury wished Rawlin could be here with him, but that was getting too personal.

The hospital attendant told him to go back to the clinic in a couple of days for the results whenever he was through. He thanked the woman and left.

In the meantime, he needed to work. He had no money, and now he had to pay Rawlin back for the clothes that he'd chosen. He decided to go out to Charles De Gaul Airport so that he wouldn't run into Rawlin. He was just walking into one of the terminals when he saw a man of about sixty looking at him as he passed.

The man was Irish and nice-looking. Amaury followed, and then whenever the man looked, he caught up with Amaury. He took Amaury into the Admiral's Club, a private men's room.

"You are legal, aren't you, boy?" Amaury said that he was twenty-one, so they sat down. "So, how much for what you do?" They were alone in the place, so Amaury spoke freely. He just hoped the man wasn't the Police.

"Everything for $100USD. The older man's eyes lit up at the 'everything' part.

"That's a lot of money for a bit of fun with a boy." Amaury gave him a wicked smile, leaned over, and whispered that he was very good at what he did and worth the price. The man smiled. "I do wish I had more time with you so that we could get a room. You could show me all the things that you do, young man. But alas, my flight won't allow it this time. We'll just go into the men's room stall at the end of the row. You go ahead, and I'll be along in a couple of minutes."

Amaury held out his hand, into which the man put $20. At least it was easy money and quick. He headed for the men's room, and shortly the Irishman joined him. He turned toward Amaury unzipped his fly.

A cow boy in Paris

By the time Amaury left the airport, he had $85US in his pocket. It's not a good night, but not a bad one either. At least he could pay Rawlin for the clothes now.

Amaury took the train to another part of the city and began to cruise. Soon, his stomach began to ache, which made his head hurt. He had to get something to eat. The drink that he'd had with Rawlin had been the last thing he'd had. He bought a Sprite and some bread, taking it outside to eat in the grass there. It didn't seem to help, so he crawled under a shrub to lie down and sleep.

Rawlin had worked for three days now and hadn't seen or heard from Amaury, except for an envelope left at the front desk, with money enclosed. It was for the clothes.

In the afternoons, whenever he got back from work, he'd take walks looking for the Amaury.

The fourth night, on a whim, he decided to go back to the tower for a drink and the view. Rawlin rode up to the second platform, drank, and headed for the top.

It was a chilly night, and the wind was blowing somewhat hard this high up. Rawlin zipped up his jacket and looked out on the beautiful city. It seemed years ago whenever Amaury had pointed out the Eiffel Tower on their first taxi ride to the hotel. God, he missed the guy. He'd been a shell of a man until they'd met.

Amaury had made him come alive in ways he had never been able to before. But now, he was gone, and his old self had returned. Work and work, nothing more. He was drowning in thought.

"You know I hear proposals are here, a lot." Rawlin broke into a smile, slowly turning around. Was he dreaming? There was Amaury, hands on his hips, smiling at him.

"Yeah, some Frenchman told me that it's because it is so romantic up here. I have to agree. But it's only romantic when you are with someone special." Rawlin held out his arms, into which Amaury ran, and fell into a passionate kiss. "Where the hell have you been? I've missed you." He kept the boy in his arms, kissing his neck, then his cheek. "And where's your jacket? It's cold up here."

"You have at your hotel. Besides, it was not cold earlier. I am fine." Rawlin took a step back, looking him over. He was not okay. He was wearing a pair of dirty brown pants and a wrinkled navy shirt. His hair was messy, and he looked pale.

"Are you fine because you don't look so good, kiddo? Why didn't you get the clothes whenever you dropped off the money?" Amaury just hugged him again. He was cold to the touch. Rawlin took off his coat, putting it around Amaury's shoulders. Amaury whispered into his ear.

"You were at work. I wouldn't ask the hotel for them. Take me with you, Rawlin." Rawlin nodded, and they headed for the elevator.

"Let's go, baby."

It was late whenever they got back to the hotel. Amaury ached and was tired and cold. Rawlin must have thought he looked like a street urchin because he did.

"Go get yourself a hot shower, baby." Amaury headed toward the bedroom. "Hey, are you hungry?" Amaury turned back. He was starving. Rawlin knew that room service was already closed for the night, so he rang the front desk.

"This is Mr. Jones. Could someone run and pick up some food at that little café close to here? I want some soup. I'll make it worth their while to go get it." Michael, the bellman who was just getting off work, would do it. He'd send him right up. "Thanks." Rawlin hung up, and Michael was knocking on the door seconds later. Rawlin told him what he wanted, gave him some money, and checked Amaury.

Amaury felt better but was still very tired. He was drying off when Rawlin came in with a pair of the underwear they'd bought at the department store. He handed them to Amaury, who put them on. Amaury then brushed his teeth and combed through his wet hair.

"You look much better. I have some food on the way up. Go get in the bed and warm up while we wait on the food to get here."

Amaury did get into bed and was soon fast asleep. He was exhausted.

Rawlin didn't want to bother Amaury, so he went into the parlor to finish the daily report while waiting for the food to arrive.

Though he wanted to take the day off to ensure Amaury got some rest, he just couldn't. Not at this stage of the project.

Whenever the food arrived, Rawlin gave Michael $50 for his trouble, and then he set the food out on a tray for Amaury and another one for himself. He carried the food into the bedroom.

Amaury was still asleep, but he needed to eat. Rawlin doubted he had eaten much lately. He was thinner than Rawlin remembered. He sat the tray on the nightstand. "Amaury, wake up, honey. You need to eat a little something, okay?" Amaury opened his eyes, yawned, and sat up. Rawlin stuffed two pillows behind his back and then sat the tray on his lap. "They didn't have any soup, so I told the bellman to get something mild if they didn't. I hope you like it." Amaury looked at the food. There was baked fish, noodles, vegetables, and some bread. Amaury took a fork and dug in. Rawlin poured Amaury a glass, then himself.

Rawlin pulled a chair over and sat next to Amaury to eat. He watched the boy, whom he tried not to star. Amaury was eating as if he hadn't eaten in days.

Rawlin broke the bread in half and buttered it. The two of them ate without talking. Amaury knew he must look like a pig to Rawlin, but he was so hungry, he didn't care. Rawlin's heart ached for him. He never wanted this boy to be dirty and hungry again. He had to do something.

"Amaury, I'd like you to stay here with me." Amaury stopped eating and looked at Rawlin. What did he mean?

"At least for a couple of nights, you know, to get some rest and to fatten you up a bit." Now Amaury understood. Why had he even thought for a moment that this man meant that he wanted him to stay with him because he loved him? "I just can't take off at the end of a job, but I want you to just think of this place as your own for the next couple of days. I want you here, okay?" Amaury studied his face.

"You want me here to convalescence, but no other reason?" Rawlins's heart ached. He picked up the bread, tearing at it, just to do something, anything.

"Amaury, I'm not very good with saying what I feel to a guy, and you know what I mean and want, baby." Amaury sighed loudly.

"Yes, but I maybe need to hear words said out loud, no matter how badly you miss it, um, mess it up. Just try for me?" Rawlin took a deep breath, thinking about how he would word it. He closed his eyes for a moment and then spoke.

"Okay, I care about you more than I ever have for anyone. I need to know that you are safe and well."

Amaury began to get emotional, no matter how hard he tried not to. He fought tears, and his throat ached. It was much more than he'd expected the cowboy to say. He thought about it a few minutes before speaking.

"I will stay at your hotel until I feel I'm not wanted or am uncomfortable, yes?" Rawlin was relieved, and it showed. He stood up and went to kiss Amaury.

"I am so happy that you're going to stay." Amaury beamed at being wanted so much. It was a long time since someone had cared about him this much.

"Merci, my cowboy. I must not overeat. I eat small amounts."

"Yes, you need to eat a little this time. The fish is very light, so it shouldn't make you sick."

They ate a bit more, then Rawlin took the food away, and then it was Rawlins turn to take a shower. Amaury would be asleep when Rawlin climbed into bed, just wearing his black briefs. He spooned the boy from behind and let himself relax and fall asleep.

## Chapter 10

Rawlin still had Amaury curled into his arms whenever the six o'clock alarm went off. He carefully slid out of bed, got dressed, and this time, it was his turn to leave a note behind.

'Sweetheart,

Please don't change your mind and go. Have no doubts that I want you here. It could be late whenever I get back. I'll phone you around one o'clock to know when to expect me. And make sure that you eat breakfast and lunch. Order room service, or go down to the restaurant. I will tell them that you'll be charging meals to the room. Order anything you like!"


Hugs Rawlin


Amaury would get up at ten-thirty, feeling much better. He brushed his teeth, then his hair, and called out for Rawlin. He then looked at the clock.

He walked into the parlor, finding the note there. It was sweet.

He was hungry again. Now, to put on some of his new clothes. He walked into the closet. Rawlin had hung up the new clothes, and they were hanging together at the end of the closet. He pulled on the jeans that he'd bought and began to look through Rawlins's clothes. He was curious as to if the cowboy wore anything but cowboy clothes.

There were two expensive suits, some Polo shirts, casual button shirts, and t-shirts. Amaury picked up the sleeve of one of Rawlins's jackets, smelling it. It had his scent, as well as the leather.

Amaury decided that he wanted to wear one of Rawlins's t-shirts. Even though it would be enormous, he picked out a red one that said, 'Texas Tech Red Raiders on it, whatever that was. He pulled it on and hugged himself. It felt good to have it on. He also grabbed a pair of socks and pulled them.

He would order room service for breakfast and then go downstairs for a late lunch. He picked up the menu, looked, and then called Room Service.

"I'd like to order a ham and cheese omelet and milk, please. Mr. Jones said to charge it to room."

"Yes, sir. The food will be here in about 15 minutes."

They'd called him sir, like a gentleman! Amaury hung up and laughed.

It had been a nice thing for Rawlin to do so that it was not an awkward situation to order room service.

Now, what to do? He looked around the suite and through the books on the coffee table. 'The Haunted Mesa' was there, as well as books by Clancy, Grisham, and a biography of James Dean. Amaury was pleased that they had similar tastes in books and men. He wondered if Rawlin had ever read a gay love story before. He'd have to get one for him. He probably didn't even know those kinds of books existed.

Amaury took 'The Haunted Mesa,' lay across the couch, and began to read it. When a knock came at the door a few moments later,

Amaury ran like a little boy, excited that his food had arrived. A charming boy about his age stood there when he opened the door. "Entre', entre,'" he told the boy. "Just place it on the bar, please." The boy did as asked. He walked back to the door, turned to give Amaury the once over, and winked. "Merci, Cheri." The boy smiled and walked out of the room.

Amaury took his meal out onto the balcony to eat. It was cool outside, not cold, but he went back inside to get his new jacket and turned on the stereo so that he could hear it out there.

He put his feet up on the other chair as he ate. He could get used to this lifestyle. He'd be keeping house and shopping while Rawlin was at work and ready whenever his lover got home.

After eating and reading out on the balcony for a while, Amaury began to feel tired and weak again. He lay on the couch to watch some TV and fell asleep.


Rawlin was so busy wrapping up the project that he didn't get around to calling the hotel until around two o'clock. The phone rang and rang. Had he decided not to stay? Finally, he picked up.

"Hello?" Amaury sat up on the couch.

"Hi, baby. How's it going?" Rawlin tried to hide that he was thrilled that Amaury had stayed.

"It is fine. I got back just now from lunch. It's fun to order all I wish!" Then he thought to add, "But I was within reason, Cheri. But they had to serve me! They call me 'sir.'" He gave Rawlin a 'take that kind of laugh, making Rawlin chuckle.

"They'd better treat you like a fucking Prince, baby. You let me know if they don't, and I'll take care of it, okay." Amaury giggled.

"Ah, Cheri, you defend my honor. Is very sweet to me." He made a 'kiss, kiss' sound into the phone." Rawlin laughed easily.

"Well, I'm glad you feel better and are enjoying yourself. I should be back around eight o'clock. Wait for me, and we'll eat dinner together. I'm sorry it will be so late, but I think we can finish up if I stay."

"Okay, I'll be here for you. I'm wearing your Teach shirt to feel closer to you. Is it okay I do this?" Rawlin was both touched and amused by this boyish gesture. "What is this Texas Teach, anyway?"

"It's Texas Tech, and that's the university where I graduated. I think it's kinda sexy that you're wearing my shirt." Rawlin became turned on by the thought.

"Oui, I think this, too." Amaury was amazed how far his cowboy had come, from the first day he'd ran away and the second, whenever he had pushed him out just for touch, in the beginning.

"Well, I've gotta get back to work, or I won't be back by eight. I'll see ya later, baby."

"Au revoir, Cheri!" They hung up feeling truly happy for the first time in a long time.


Later, on the ride back to the hotel, Rawlin was nervous for several reasons. Was he getting himself into a situation that he couldn't handle? Just what was he planning on happening with this guy, or did he even have to worry about it? Amaury might pull one of those disappearing acts of his, get angry and leave, to get out of the situation altogether. He'd find out soon enough.

Rawlin could hear music from inside as he walked up to the hotel door. After a few tries, he got the card to work and came inside. Amaury was lying on the couch reading. The music was so loud that he hadn't even heard Rawlin come in. Rawlin walked over to the stereo, turning down the volume, and then to Amaury, who had sat up now. He closed the book, got up, and kissed Rawlin.

"I am glad you are back." Rawlin pulled him into his arms for a proper kiss.

"I was so afraid that you'd be gone, and all I'd have is one of your notes, again."

"I'm famished. Are you?" Rawlin was, but he wanted to shower and change before they went out, so he headed for the bathroom. Amaury lay back on the couch and returned to his novel while waiting.

Rawlin was happy. Happy that Amaury was still there. He took a quick shower and put on a pair of relaxed jeans and a hunter green Polo shirt. Instead of boots, he put on his black Adidas sneakers. He was leaving his shirt un-tucked and putting some gel on his hair to make it wavier. He walked into the parlor.

"I'm ready to go, babe. Let's go get something to eat." Amaury jumped up.

"I'm changing shirts first. This one is too big for general wear, I'm afraid." He went into the bedroom, returning with the yellow and green 'OUI' shirt. "I'm ready now." He slipped on his loafers, and they headed for the elevator, arm in arm.

"Where are we going, anyway? You got any ideas, kiddo?" Amaury hated when Rawlin called him a kid. He hadn't been one in a long time.

"You miss American. I know a place." They headed across the lobby and into the night.

"Why the hell not! I haven't had American in a while." He then looked at Amaury with suspicion. "It's not

## A cow boy in Paris

McDonald's, is it?" Amaury broke into a fit of laughter. No, he had another place in mind where Rawlin would feel right at home.

They headed for the metro station and discussed their day.

Amaury told Rawlin how he'd enjoyed staying in such a nice place, and Rawlin told him that the Rouen job was almost complete and how successful it had been. "We'll get a bonus out of this one for sure. Saved the company a lot of money, the way we did it." Amaury loved hearing Rawlin talk about anything. His use of language and the sexy Texas accent were entertaining to him.

The train pulled to a stop, and the two of them got off and walked on the street. The Texas-Style Café was right across the metro entrance and was decorated in Texas neon signs.

"Well now, this is my kind of place, if the food is good." They walked inside to a booth in the corner. There was an oil derrick with a fountain at the top so that it looked like a gusher. Rawlin sat on one side, and to his surprise, Amaury sat next to him, on the same side. He put his hand on Rawlins's knee. Rawlin looked around nervously.

"Vous etes une ame marvelleus, Rawlin. Merci d' etre si aimable avec mio." Rawlin got most of it, but Amaury then translated it to make sure he understood. Amaury was giving Rawlin a kiss when the waiter appeared.

"Bonjour et bienauenue! Que des garons Vousdrez-vous boire?" Amaury looked to Rawlin to place his order.

"You are the real Texan, so you order for us." Rawlin bashfully grinned ducked his head. "And speak English for the cowboy, please. His French is only a bit." The waiter nodded and waited as Rawlin looked at the menu. Now, to impress both of them, Rawlin ordered in French.

"Oui, nous voulons tous les deux pienous le bifteck frit der poutlet." The waiter wrote it down and left them alone. Amaury squeezed his arm.

"That was very good. Your French is improving! Can you speak other languages?" Rawlin told him that he could speak Spanish, which he'd learned in school and working in the oil fields, and a bit of Arabic and German from working in those countries.

"We learn multiple languages in school, not work as you mostly do. Which countries have you been to, and do you like France the best?" The waiter returned with two glasses of iced tea.

"The first place I went, overseas, was to Saudi." He sipped his tea. "Whoa! That's sweet tea!" A few people were in the place, so Rawlin got braver and put his arm around Amaury. "I've been to Belgium, the United Kingdom, Spain, Brazil, Russia, Norway, Germany, the U.A.E., Columbia, Pakistan, Iran, Canada, Amsterdam, Australia, Fiji, South Africa, and Indonesia. I think that's it. Oh, wait, I've been to China, too." He leaned against Amaury. "I do like it here, so it is one of my favorite places. That may have more to do with the people here, though." He winked at Amaury.

The food soon arrived. Amaury looked at his place, took his fork, and peeled back the crust a bit. "It's Chicken Fried Steak. It's just a piece of beef battered with flour and egg, and then they fry it up and put crème gravy on it. Try it." They also had traditional fried potatoes, pinto beans, and French toast. Rawlin took a bite. He had to admit, and it was pretty damned good. Amaury seemed to like it, too. "My mother makes this all the time. She has the best I've ever tasted, but this is not bad at all, for Paris, France!"

"You have food fried a lot in Texas, then?" Rawlin laughed. Yes, they did, and it was a wonder he didn't weigh 300 pounds!

"My mom had lots of fruit and veggies, too, because we grew them on the farm in our garden. Guess that's what saved me from having clogged arteries. That and I was always running around everywhere or riding my horses."

Amaury sat down his fork, his eyes lighting up.

"You had horses of your own? You are a true cowboy?" Rawlin agreed that yes, he was the real deal.

"Yeah, we had horses. We all did. We do."

After they ate, Rawlin complimented the chef and found out that he was a Texan who had met a French woman on vacation in Paris, and he just stayed and then opened the café.

Rawlin and Amaury decided to take a walk along the Seine. He'd wanted to do this with Amaury since he'd begun to have feelings for him. So they headed for the metro again and got off not far from the famous river.

They walked down to Amaury's footpath hooked his arm in Rawlins. The moon was almost complete. It indeed was romantic and beautiful.

They walked for a while, seeing other couples doing the same thing and some same-sex couples, making Rawlin feel a little less obvious.

When they approached the bridge, Amaury pulled Rawlin into the darkness of the bridge overhead, kissing him. They kissed for a while and then continued their walk. Amaury told Rawlin a bit of history as they walked, but he soon began to feel light-headed and nauseous. He tried to ignore it, but finally, he had to stop.

"I need to sit a moment, Rawlin." Rawlin led him to a bench a little distance away, where they sat. Amaury closed his eyes, holding his stomach.

"What's wrong, baby?" Amaury began to rock back and forth, making Rawlin even more concerned. "Tell me what's wrong."

"Je ne me sens pas si bon." Amaury held his arms across his stomach. (I don't feel so well.) "Je sais melody a monestomac." Now he tried to sit still, hoping the aching would stop. It didn't.

"I guess the food didn't agree with you. Probably because you aren't used to that grease." Amaury nodded. Maybe that's all it was.

They sat there for a while, and then Amaury was able to head back to the hotel. They walked to the metro, boarded, and as they rode, Amaury rested his head on Rawlins's head. The rocking of the rail car did nothing to help Amaury out, so he held his stomach.

By the time they got back to the hotel room, Amaury's stomach was much worse. Rawlin found his stomach medicine, giving some to Amaury. Amaury slowly undressed and climbed into bed. The medication did calm his stomach, and he fell asleep.

When Amaury awoke, he felt fine. The aches and pains were all gone. He looked over at Rawlin, who was snoring lightly. Amaury smiled at his chest as he just peeked out from the covers. It was almost bare.

Amaury carefully pulled back the covers to not wake Rawlin seeing the outline in Rawlins's briefs. He moved up, lightly kissing Rawlins lips as his hand trailed down the chest, teasing at the underwear band. Rawlin woke and moaned. Amaury's caresses worked on down to Rawlins's thighs.

"Morning. You must be feeling better." Amaury looked up at him, smiling.

"Oui and I want to play. Please don't stop me this time. It's okay."

Rawlin was terrified but said nothing. He didn't think he could speak if he'd wanted to. Amaury's hands found their way down Rawlin's body. Rawlin gasped and closed his eyes. When Rawlin didn't stop him, Amaury began to pleasure Rawlin in a way he'd never experienced before. This guy knew what he was doing and was very good at it. Amaury loved the power of pleasing a man and controlling how they reacted. But for Rawlin, he just wanted to please him, and he did much more than that.

Finished, Amaury crawled up and lay on top of Rawlin. He was so light, and it was perfect. Rawlin put his arms around the boy, caressing his back.

"No wonder you do so well working the streets. That was amazing!" Amaury laughed, and Rawlin held him tighter to his body. "And if you ask me if I'm glad you stayed again, I'll kick your cute ass out of this bed!" They both laughed.

Rawlin began to tickle Amaury's sides, holding him down. Amaury finally worked his way loose and sat beside Rawlin. He pulled the boy back into his arms, kissing him. As Rawlin looked up at Amaury and his heart swelled.

The wake-up call broke the spell. "Hell, I've gotta go to work." Rawlin sat up, groaning. He walked to the shower and got inside. He was still riding a high of what had happened that he did not want to leave for work today. He had no choice.

Bummed, Rawlin turned the water temperature a bit colder. He was amazed by what he had let happen. He'd let a guy pleasure him, and it was the best he'd ever had. He was picking up the soap when Amaury joined him. They began to lather one another, caressing every part of their bodies. It was very sensual and frustrating at the same time for Rawlin. "I should be back from Rouen early today. Then I've got to check on the next job and find out when I have to be there." They rinsed off and got out of the shower, dried off, and got dressed.

"So, I'm on my own for lunch? I want to go out today. I'll be easy on myself, don't worry."

"Yes, you are on your own for lunch, but do you need to go out? There's good food right here at the hotel."

"I need fresh air and sunshine. Is good for my health." Rawlin couldn't argue with that.

Today, Rawlin dressed in his gray suit pants and a white button shirt with a red tie. Instead of the matching jacket, he wore a thin, black leather. When Amaury saw him, the boy whistled. He walked over to Rawlin, kissing him. "Do you realize just how sexy you are, cowboy? I think not, but you are, indeed." Amaury, who only had red boy shorts, pulled him closer and kissed Rawlin again. Rawlin suddenly had a thought. He held Amaury at arm's length.

"You aren't going hustling today, are you? Is that why you need to go out?" Amaury scowled and pulled away. He put on his jeans, glaring at Rawlin.

"It's what I do, Rawlin, and no, I was not going to hustle today, but it's my choice, my freedom, you understand? Is my choice, not yours, if I do."

Rawlin just shook his head, found his briefcase, and headed for the door. He stopped there, going back. Amaury was looking for his bag.

"I'm sorry. I didn't mean it that way. I'm sorry." Rawlin realized that he might not want Amaury to hustle that he was jealous.

When Amaury didn't respond, stuffing his belongings into his bag, Rawlin got angry with him. To hell with him, then! Wouldn't he even accept an apology?

Rawlin got out his wallet, throwing some bills onto the bed. "There ya go, kid. That's for the work or whatever, this morning." He stormed out of the room.

"Asshole!" Amaury yelled after him, but as soon as he heard the hotel room door slam, he threw himself onto the bed, sobbing.

Impossible. It was an impossible situation! Every time they got close, one or the other would get scared, for their reasons, and back away.

In the elevator, Rawlin got even angrier. "Damn it!" The woman sharing the space with him was shocked. "Sorry." When the doors opened, he practically ran through the lobby.

Up in the room, Amaury had cried himself to sleep and finished getting dressed. He sat there wondering what to do and headed for the street. He was hungry, so he bought a pastry and an espresso, eating it as he walked.

It was a sunny day, and a light breeze blew his hair from his face. He went to the rail station, heading out to Marais, Paris's center of gay life.

## Chapter 11

In a park there, he sat, cross-legged, under a tree, watching the people pass by. He hadn't been there long when someone stopped, calling his name. Amaury looked up to see a fellow hustler named Jean-Marc, who sat on the ground, too.

"How are you, my old friend?" They hugged. "I haven't seen you for a long time. Where have you been, and what are you doing?"

"Oh, you know, I work, I play, and this and that. You?" Jean-Marc told him about his aunt. She had offered to pay his way through University if he quit hustling.

"But is this what you want to do?" Amaury asked him.

"Well, I plan to tell her that I stopped hustling and will go to school, but no, I never stop. It is in my blood now. I can't do a day job as the other people."

Amaury wondered if that was him, too. Had he become so accustomed to this life that he would never quit picking up men? He didn't know.

"But what if you find a man and fall in love? Would you stop then?" It was an honest question, Amaury thought, but Jean-Marc laughed.

"Would you love me, darling? No. I've been on the streets since I was twelve years old, hustling. No one wants to keep a boy such as us, Amaury."

"But just say that it did happen one day, this love. Would you quit?" The boy patted Amaury on the back and then thought about it for a moment.

"Yes, you romantic dreamer, I would quit if I found this true love of which you speak. I would hustle no longer." The comment made Amaury feel better.

The two young men spent the morning just walking around talking. They had a cheap lunch, and then they went into a bookstore there in Marais. Amaury thought about the fight he'd had with Rawlin. He felt terrible about it.

Amaury decided to get something for Rawlin as a peace offering. He looked around the store and then remembered that he'd wanted to get Rawlin a gay romance novel. He looked through the books, deciding on Maurice. It was the perfect mix of accepting who you are and love.

Amaury was looking for a gift bag whenever Jean-Marc found him.

"Getting some hot reading, darling?" He leaned his head on Amaury's shoulder. "I've read that book. It's delicious!"

"It's not for me. It's for a man I know. I just need to get a gift bag. Where are they?" Jean-Marc led the way.

"I'll wait for you outside. I have what I need if you know what I mean." He opened his jacket just enough to let Amaury see the two books he had stashed there. Amaury nodded. He was glad that Jean-Marc was walking on without him since he'd stolen the books. Amaury was glad he no longer did this.

"I won't be very long."

Jean-Marc walked out the door with his bounty while Amaury headed for the cashier. The older man rang up his purchases, smiling at him.

"Merci, for paying this time." He winked at Amaury, who nervously smiled back. So the owner had known they were stealing from him. Amaury thanked him and hurried outside and across the street to Jean-Marc.

"So you pay for your things now? No more free goodies?" Amaury tied a knot in the top of the bag.

"I try not to steal anymore, Jean-Marc. I understand why you do since I did it too." His friend just shrugged.

"Hey, I've got a room at my aunt's house now. Let's go spend the afternoon together in bed!" The two boys locked arms and headed for the house.

## Chapter 12

Rawlin finished his part of the job in Rouen. At least he wouldn't have to take this daily trip any longer. He got back to Paris around two o'clock, phoning the hotel room on the way back. No one answered.

Rawlin scolded himself. He'd acted like a stupid, jealous kid, having a temper tantrum. What an idiot! His feelings were all mixed up. Guess he'd just have to go back to the hotel and see if Amaury was even there to deal with anymore. He had no idea what to expect.

When he got back to the room, it was empty. There was no sweet note this time, just buzzing quietness. Rawlin plopped down on the couch, figuring he'd better check in with the office. George was not there, so he told Marie that his job was complete.

Where would he be going next? Rawlin prayed the answer had changed. She told him that the Montreal job was waiting for him, and George would be calling him soon about it.

### A cowboy in Paris

Amaury was not returning to the hotel tonight because he was punishing Rawlin.

After taking a shower, Rawlin put on some more comfortable clothes. He needed a drink and something substantial. He poured himself a glass of straight whiskey, downed it, and poured himself another. He was just sitting down with it when someone knocked on the door.

Amaury had come back after all. Rawlin hurried to the door, opened it, saying, "I'm sorry I was such a...." He stopped mid-sentence. There stood George Akin, the boss of his company. Rawlin was very surprised to see him. "George, what in the world are you doing here? We finished the job today."

"I know. I went to Rouen before I came over here. You need to answer your phone, Rawlin." Rawlin just stood there. "Can I come in?" Rawlin came out of his stupor and moved to the side.

"Yes, of course. Come on in and have a seat. I'm having a drink. You want something?" George wanted whatever he was having, so Rawlin poured him a glass and handed it to the man. "So, we were almost perfect on this job, as I'm sure they told you. They're thrilled with us." Rawlin sat on the arm of the couch.

"Yeah, they are happy. Cedric wants you for every job their outfit does now. Good work. You are the best at what you do, Jones." The two men drank their whiskey.

"So why did you fly over here when you knew I had everything in hand, George? What's going on?" The older man sat his glass down.

"That's what I'm trying to figure out. You refuse a job, and then you don't check in with me or answer your phone. You left me no choice but to come over here, Rawlin. Irresponsible behavior is not like you at all. Is it this woman you've met? Is that it?"

"It's not a woman. I haven't met a woman, George. I just needed some time off, and I took it. I called the office earlier, and Marie told me you were out. I had planned to go to Montreal at the end of the week. I just need to know when I'll be working back here, in Europe. I don't want to work in North America."

"You didn't call your parents, did you? They're really worried about you, too."

Rawlin got up to get himself another drink. He was so tired of everyone being so worried about him.

"I'm as fine as a man can be after going through what I have, and now I have to come to terms with who I am, George. Maybe I can't go home right now."

George began telling him how helpful family can be when a knock at the door interrupted them. Oh, hell! Please don't let it be Amaury. But it was, and he began to bang on the door.

"Rawlin, I'm back! Answer the door." He began to speak in French, thank goodness, as Rawlin ran for the door, almost tripping as he did so. He threw open the door, blocking the way into the room. "Cheri, I'm back. I bring you a peace offering, okay?" He held the bag toward Rawlin, who took it. Amaury was acting very strangely and talking very loudly. Rawlin shushed him and whispered back.

"Could you lower your voice, damn it? My boss is in here. You can't come in. Go somewhere and come back in about an hour." Amaury was confused. He tried to kiss Rawlin. "Stop it! What's the matter with you? You're high on something, aren't you?" Amaury broke into giggles.

"I have a little pick me up, Oui. Is just for fun, not hustling, okay? I run into an old friend and..." Rawlin practically put his hand over Amaury's mouth, stepping out into the hall with him.

"Amaury, do you want me to lose my job? Because that's what's going to happen if you don't shut up and go somewhere for just a little while. I'm sorry I was such a jealous jerk before, but please, just go for a while." Amaury looked so hurt. "Sweetheart, please do this for me. Please," he pleaded.

Amaury was sobering up quickly. He could see the panic in Rawlins's eyes.

"I will go, Rawlin, because you are begging of me to go, but I won't be back tonight, perhaps ever." He turned to go down toward the elevator. Rawlin went after him.

"It's not so easy for me, Amaury. Please try to understand and don't hate me for doing this. I just have to take care of a few business things, and then we'll talk about this drug thing." Amaury scoffed at him, annoyed.

"What I do when I am without you is none of your business, Rawlin." He slipped into the elevator, and the doors closed before Rawlin could say anything more.

He hurried back to his hotel room and went inside, tossing the gift bag on the bar.

George had poured himself another drink and stood by the liquor cabinet when he came back in. Rawlin was upset, and it showed. The last thing he wanted to do was talk about work and when or if he was going to Montreal or Texas. He sat in the chair, leaned back, and sighed. George came back over and sat on the couch.

"Who was that, Rawlin?" Rawlin looked at him. He could just see what would happen if he said that was his lover at the door, and he was a nineteen-year-old young man who hustled for a living. He was a little high, and I'm embarrassed that I'm gay, so I sent him out into the streets. What if he did? Geez! Is everything alright?

"He's just someone I met here in Paris, George." He had to get his boss out of the hotel and Paris. He'd do whatever it took to accomplish that. "I will be in Montreal on Friday, George, and go home for Christmas. I'll call my mother. Everything is just perfect. Just tell me when I can come back to Europe, will you?" He needed to know now that he had to go to North America.

"We've got a couple of jobs coming up in Belgium after New Year's. You're the perfect man for the job, Rawlin. And I'm sure that you'll like your Christmas and end-of-year bonus' coming up. You've earned it, Jones." George stood up, as did Rawlin. They shook hands. "Take care of yourself, Rawlin. You look tired."

They walked to the door together.

"I'm trying to, George. I'm trying to do that and make everyone around me happy, too." George patted him on the back.

"I'll see you in Montreal. I'll go on over and get things started up for you."

"Thanks, George. I appreciate it."

Back in the room, Rawlin sat in the chair, thinking. The room was too quiet. He knew what he had to do. He grabbed his coat and headed for the street.

Amaury could still feel the buzz as he walked down the street, but his heart ached, too. Rawlin had kicked him out onto the street. Yes, he'd been stupid enough to show up high at his door, but he'd wanted to apologize to Rawlin. He didn't know what to think of what Rawlin had done. He'd been ashamed of him and afraid it would cost him his job.

It was hard for Amaury to understand how it must feel—he'd never been ashamed of being gay. He tried to think of it from Rawlins's point of view. He walked down to a café, ordering an espresso there.

He was still sitting there, drinking his second cup, when Rawlin found him. Without a word, he sat at the table with Amaury. He ordered a coffee.

"I' m sorry, Amaury. I'm sorry about being jealous before and sad about having to ask you to leave. I didn't know what else to do. I'm sorry." He reached across the table, taking one of Amaury's hands. He didn't pull away.

"Why are you so afraid to be queer, Rawlin? It's not a disease or sickness, you know? It's just who you are and who you love. Nothing to fear."

Rawlin admired how confidently Amaury said the words.

"I am deathly afraid of it, to be honest. It's ingrained in my head that being gay is wrong. It's a sin. I fight that with all of my beings, but I still have a ways to go." He squeezed Amaury's hand. "You have helped me so much. Help me get the rest of the way there. Don't give up on me, and I won't give up on you." This last statement made Amaury cry silent tears and move to hug Rawlin.

"I am an asshole, with you earlier today. I am too defensive sometimes. I have to fight my own family for myself, remembering? You help me, too."

Rawlin kissed Amaury. He didn't care who saw it. "Oh, and I don't take drugs, but this time it's with an old friend, not hustling. It's stupid of me to do. I won't again."

Rawlin was glad to hear it. He was worried this was a common thing Amaury did.

"So, we're okay?" Amaury nodded. "Let's go back to the room."

The two of them walked back to the room, where they went to bed, making out and falling asleep in one another's arms.

Rawlin didn't see Amaury again until late the following night. When he came in, Amaury asked him about the gift. Rawlin had forgotten all about the bag. He went to get it from the bar and brought it back to the bed, where Amaury sat. "Is just something to educate you, cowboy." The grin on the boy's face made Rawlin very curious. He opened the bag and the card. It said, 'Veuillez ne pas me tourner parti, Rawlins' xxoo, Amaury.' "It says to please don't turn me away." Rawlin got emotional, nodded, and took the book from the bag. He read the summary on the back and smiled.

"Thank you. I'll read it right away." It was nice and somehow made things seem like more of a possibility.

"There are many books and movies of gay love these days. We are not alone in these feelings, Rawlin. Many men are attracted to other men, in many stages."

"Yeah, I'm beginning to understand that. And I guess queers want to read novels about their lifestyle too." Amaury moved closer, kissing him.

"Have you showered yet?" Rawlin hadn't. "I need to shower. Join me, Cheri. It will be fun!" Rawlin began to unbutton his shirt, so Amaury began to undress as well.

Amaury took the soap in the shower and began to lather Rawlins body. It was very sexy. Rawlin took the bar of soap and began to lather Amaury's body, too. The water fell over them as hands caressed one another.

Afterward, they dried off before heading to bed. Whenever Rawlin started to pull on his briefs, Amaury stopped him. He was right. It was time they slept naked together. Amaury curled up next to his body, using Rawlins arm as a pillow.

"This is like a dream for me, to be here with you so wonderful to me." He snuggled closer. "No faites pas un grand distribueer de lui, mais etes demain mon annwasarie." Rawlin looked down at him. Had he heard the boy right?

"You'll be twenty tomorrow? Is that what you said?" Amaury was impressed. Rawlin was getting much better with the language.

"Oui, I will be twenty tomorrow. Another birthday for me."

"Why didn't you say something about it? I'd have made plans. We just have to do something special. It's a special day!" Amaury gave him an edgy look.

"I won't go overboard. It should be your choice, anyway. It's your day!"

"I will have to think on it tonight. It does not matter as long as I am spending it with you, Cheri." They kissed once more and then slept. Again, Amaury would stay the whole night with Rawlin.

## Chapter 13

The first thing Amaury wanted to do on his birthday was sleep late, so he did. It was okay with Rawlin because he had a chance to call the office and be back again, spooning the boy. He never knew Rawlin had left the bed.

Rawlin didn't sleep for a while. He listened to Amaury breathing and enjoyed holding him. Then he let himself fall back to sleep.

Up by eleven, they got dressed, and Amaury insisted on wearing the Texas Tech Red Raiders shirt again. He tied it up at the bottom so that it looked sexy on him, even though it was too big. They ate breakfast downstairs. The staff no longer gave Amaury nasty looks. They treated him just like a genuine guest.

"Well, happy birthday, baby." They kissed and toasted with their coffee. "So, what did you decide that you wanted to do?"

"I wish to spend the day in Marais." Rawlin had heard of the area of town but wasn't sure what was there to see, but it was Amaury's decision.

"What's there?" Amaury told him that the area was on the right bank where, in the seventeenth century, Henri IV built 'place des Vosges, attracting wealthy aristocrats to the site. When they all moved to Versailles, ordinary Parisians had taken over the area.

Today, it was a trendy community filled with diverse peoples, art galleries, antique shops, eateries, bars, and Revolutionary architecture.

It sounded terrific to Rawlin, so they finished eating, took the metro to the Saint Paul Station, and walked the neighborhood. Amaury talked as they went along.

"Victor Hugo once lived in this house here. It is now a museum. That one is Muse' Carnavalet, the Paris History Museum."

"This is the Jewish settlement and the gay area." They went into all of the arcades along the way, taking their time. And at lunchtime, they ate in a quaint little café sharing a giant sandwich. Then they were on their way once again.

He stopped to look at Rawlin for his reaction. He looked like it was okay. "This is the reason I bring you here. It is beautiful and diverse. I love it here."

Rawlin was suddenly aware of other same-sex couples walking around the neighborhood. He took Amaury's hand, locking fingers with him. Amaury's heart warmed.

They would stop here and there during their day and then include a trip to the Musee Picasso on the way before ending up standing outside The Open Bar. "This is where I chose to eat dinner. Is a popular hangout for gays." Rawlin looked suspicious. "A meeting place, not a cruising one."

They walked into the place, and a waiter took them to a booth. Amaury slid in and was happy whenever Rawlin sat on the same side of the booth with him, without protest. Why the hell not, Rawlin thought. It's the gay neighborhood, after all. He couldn't possibly run into anyone he knew here. A thought came to his mind.

"Cruising. Is that looking for a guy to be with?" Amaury laughed and kissed his cheek.

"If you think it is looking for a man to have sex with, then yes, cruising is just what you think, Cheri." Rawlin nodded, put his arm around the boy, and kissed him. It was not just a peck this time, but a good kiss. Amaury was so happy. His cowboy was not so afraid here in the gay scene. "After we eat, we go next door to the club to dance." Rawlin groaned at the word 'dance.'

"Just what kind of dancing are we talking about, honey?" Amaury ran a hand up Rawlins's thigh and across him.

"House or techno music with beautiful gay men dancing and sweaty!"

Amaury could tell that Rawlin was not too happy about the idea.

"Baby, if all the boys are as young and sexy as you are, then I'll pass. I'll look like an idiot out there. I'll just watch you dance." The waiter appeared, and Rawlin tried to order champagne, but Amaury insisted on wine.

"Non, non, they're all men ages there. You will see. I don't wish to dance with anyone but you, cowboy, on my birthday. You say it is my choice." The waiter returned with the wine. Rawlin raised his glass and toasted to dancing.

They drank more wine, ordered the special of stuffed pork, and headed for the club.

It was a prominent place. There was a long bar that stretched along the front wall. An area of couches and chairs had couples making out in them, and there was a giant disco lighted dance floor, with lots of shirtless men dancing to an electronic beat. "Come, we sit over here. We will watch the boys."

Amaury led him to a red couch. Rawlin sat and pulled Amaury into his lap. "See? I tell you, there are men of all ages here." He was right. There were even some men who had to be older than him. It made Rawlin feel more at ease.

"Baby, the only dancing I've done in a long time is a western or slow dance. I may be a little bit rusty." Amaury put his arms around his neck, kissing him as the waiter appeared.

"Boys, Que des garcons Voudrez-vous boire?" They broke apart, laughing.

"Sure," Rawlin said. "He'll have a Cosmo, and I want a rum and coke, please." The waiter nodded, telling them to resume kissing, and they did.

After a few more drinks, Amaury managed to get Rawlin out onto the dance floor. Rawlin surprised himself by catching on pretty quickly for a cowboy.

They wouldn't make it back to the hotel until around eleven-thirty. Rawlin didn't want to get in too late because he had a surprise waiting for Amaury's birthday.

As they walked past the front desk, Rawlin signaled the night attendant. Taking this as his queue, he took care of things.

In the room, Amaury hugged and kissed Rawlin.

"What a day! Merci bouquet." They kissed again, and then there was a knock at the door.

"It's not quite over yet, baby. Just have a seat on the couch, there." Rawlin went to the door and rolled a cart inside with a cake and a chilled bottle of champagne. He found the lighter he'd purchased on the bar and lit the candles. He simultaneously pushed the cart to Amaury, singing, 'Happy Birthday .' simultaneously. Amaury loved it! Rawlin stopped right in front of him. "Now close your eyes make a wish, and then you have to blow all of the candles out at one time for your wish to come true." Amaury closed his eyes, made his wish, and then blew. All of the candles went out, and they both clapped and then kissed. Rawlin cut the white cake with pink roses and 'Happy Birthday Amaury' written pink.

Amaury took a finger full of frosting and fed it to Rawlin, who sucked his finger seductively. Rawlin sat on the couch with Amaury.

"Thank you, once again, Rawlin, for my beautiful day. It means so much to me." They kissed as Rawlin found the gift he'd hid behind one of the pillows earlier. He handed it to Amaury. "This is not needed, Rawlin. The day and the cake, they were enough." He tore off the paper and opened the box. Inside was a gold necklace with a heart locket on it. It was costly and beautiful. Amaury began to tear up.

"There's an inscription inside. Open it up and read it." Amaury opened up the locket. It read, 'You are always in my heart. Love, Cowboy.' Amaury's hand went to his heart. He couldn't speak. He was so moved as the tears fell down his face. When he looked at Rawlin, he was crying too. It was a big moment.

"Je t'aime advantage que n' import quoi dans le monde, cowboy." He didn't translate this time, for he was saying to himself, more than to Rawlin. 'I love you more than anything in the world.'

"Let's see how it looks on your sexy neck." He took the necklace from Amaury, who turned round where Rawlin could clasp it at the back of his neck. He raised his hair, and then Rawlin put it on. He kissed the boy's neck, and then Amaury turned back around. They kissed again, and then Amaury went to the nearby mirror. It was so beautiful. He walked back to Rawlin, who rose.

"It is perfect, my cowboy. I just need one more thing for my birthday, Rawlin Jones." He cupped Rawlins chin gently into his hand. "Make love to me, Rawlin."

# Chapter 14

The morning sun woke him. Rawlin carefully got out of bed to make a quick call. Amaury was awake whenever he returned. He lay back on the bed.

"Good morning, baby." He kissed Amaury. "I'm gonna take a shower." He got up and headed for the shower. Amaury thought of joining him, but he also wanted to just lay there in bed, taking in the memories of the day and night before. It had been perfect. His hand went to the locket around his neck. Lost in a daydream, he barely heard Rawlin yell to him that it was his turn in the shower. He slid out of bed and walked into the bathroom.

"Can we go to the opera one night? I love the opera. It is a magnificent experience." Rawlin just scowled at him as he pulled on a pair of briefs.

"You've gone to the opera?" Amaury nodded.

"Oui, I go many times at the Palais Garnier. It's world-famous. This man I know sometimes takes me." He got into the shower as Rawlin put his toothbrush into his mouth. "So can we go?" Rawlin rinsed out his mouth.

"I've never been. I never even thought of going. So I can't say that I don't like it." Rawlin walked out to get some clothes. Amaury was out of the shower when he came back. He began to brush his teeth.

"That is true, that you don't know if you've never been. The experience alone is beautiful, even if you don't care for the music and singing." Rawlin headed out to get his socks and boots on. He was sitting on the bed when Amaury came out and sat on the bed, naked. He was humming something.

"Get dressed, sweetie, and then come out to the parlor. We still have your birthday cake waiting for us. We'll have some for breakfast." Rawlin headed out into the other room. While Amaury dressed, Rawlin got out some plates forks and checked the bottle of champagne on the cart. The ice had kept it chilled through the night, so he grabbed a couple of glasses. He cut the cake and put some onto the plates.

Amaury was in Rawlins closet. He looked through the clothes and chose another shirt. This one said, 'Native Texan' on it. It was grey with Texas on it, colored like the flag. He pulled on his older jeans and came into the parlor barefooted. Rawlin looked up at him in his wet hair and oversized shirt.

"You're so damned cute." Amaury smiled and sat next to him. "Let's eat some of this cake, shall we? We kinda got busy last night and forgot about it."

Amaury grinned sheepishly and took the plate Rawlin held out to him. He took a bite. It was good.

"I never have this birthday cake with the candles. Is pretty fun." Rawlin ate a bite of his cake and then figured it might as well tell Amaury what was about to happen. He took a drink of the champagne first.

"Amaury, I need to talk to you about something serious." Amaury watched Rawlin's face and quickly put his plate down. "You know that I'm finished with the job in Rouen, right?" Amaury nodded. "It's almost the holidays, and the New Year is coming up. In my business, well, it means a lot of things."

Amaury was feeling light-headed. He knew what was coming. He should have listened to his head, not his heart. Of course, it would happen, eventually.

"Just tell me." Rawlin nodded. This news was going to be the hardest thing he'd ever had to say in his life.

"They're sending me to another job, baby. It's all set up for me, and I've already put it off to be with you as long as I could." He reached for Amaury's hand, but he pulled away. "I'll be back as soon as I can. I told my boss, the one you saw in the hotel here with me, that I only want to work in the Eastern Hemisphere from now on."

Rawlin was getting sadder, and he could see Amaury was getting angry. His jaw was clenched tighter. He glared at the Texan. "It gets slow at this time of year, and...." Amaury interrupted him.

"Where and when?" He crossed his arms across his chest, and his knee bounced up and down with emotion. Rawlin could hardly speak.

"They're sending me to Montreal, Amaury. I have to be there on Friday, and I promised to spend Christmas with my family. I haven't been home in three years."

Amaury thought he would be working in Europe, and Rawlin could take him along. What a fool he was! Suddenly, he thought of something. He had to ask Rawlin a question.

"How long have you known, cowboy?" Rawlin had hoped he wouldn't ask this, but he wouldn't lie. Amaury would see right through him.

"A week or so, for sure, baby. I just didn't want to ruin these last days, and I wasn't sure I had to go until George came over here to tell me."

Amaury shook his head and then held it in his hands. He tried so hard not to cry. Rawlin put a hand on his back, rubbing it. Amaury looked over and then back down at the once beautiful cake was ruined. The night was nothing to him. And this cake somehow seemed a symbol of it all to him. It stood for abandonment.

Amaury closed his eyes and held still for a moment. When he opened them, he saw the label on the champagne in the ice bucket.

ROUSSEAU stared back at him. It sent him over the edge.

"Vous abruti! Hier e'tait tout pour au revoir, wasn't il? Vous vous sentez de'sole' pour laisser le de'brouillard de rue ainsi le sortir pour son anniversaire, le donnez ce qu'il veut, et puis le laissez!" Rawlin caught the jest of it all.

"No, it wasn't like that at all, Amaury. This is not goodbye. I work all over Europe, and I told you that I will only be working over here after the New Year."

"The New Year? It gets worse! You did all this," he gestured over the cake and champagne, "and you finally are not so scared a man to have sex with me. Then you leave!"

With one arm, Amaury swiped the cake off the table. It flew all over them, the floor, and the wall. He stood up and grabbed the bottle of champagne. "And this, once again, has a part to destroy my chance to happiness!" He burst the bottle in half against the coffee table, sending glass flying. Rawlin, a bit in shock over what was happening, protected his face. "Re toumez a la maison a votre proper monde, cowboy du Texas!" Rawlin knew he was telling him to go back to his closeted world in Texas. He jerked the shirt over his head and threw it at Rawlins's face. "I hate you for this! I hate you!" He ran for the door and out of the hotel room, with Rawlin running after him. He was still stunned over Amaury's reaction to his news.

"Amaury, please come back! I'm going to get you a place to live, baby!"

Amaury took the stairs, knowing that Rawlin wouldn't be able to keep up with him. He was down and onto the street before Rawlin made it out the exit door. He just caught sight of Amaury running away, barefooted and chested, down the road.

Rawlin ran a few more feet and then realized he would never catch him. He walked back to the hotel and sat on the curb. "Damn it!" He held his head down, crying like a boy, for a while. An employee walked over to ask him if he was okay. He looked up at the woman. "No, no, I'm not." He got up and walked back into the hotel and up to his room.

The room was a mess. Rawlin sat down and sobbed some more, and then he began to clean up. He found a broom and dustpan, doing the best that he could. Then he attacked it with a wet towel. He had to pick up the glass from the champagne bottle carefully. He sat the unbroken half bottle of Champagne into the dustpan.

"Happy birthday, baby." Rawlin put the glass into the trash and went to bed, laying down on it, boots and all. No more tears would come. Perhaps he'd cried himself out. He didn't know. What he did know was that his heart was breaking. He closed his eyes, and finally, he slept.

## Chapter 15

Rawlin only had three days to find Amaury before leaving for Montreal. There was no way he could cancel on George again and expect to keep his job. He just had to let Amaury know that he had planned to rent an apartment for him here in Paris so that he could get off of the streets.

But after two days without any sign of Amaury, Rawlin was panicking. He'd gone to every rail station they'd been to, the Eifel Tower, and walked along the Seine hoping he'd see the boy sketching there. He wasn't. Today, he headed for a print store so that he could get the photos that he'd taken with Amaury whenever they'd spent the day together printed. He planned to use one of them to show people, to ask if they'd seen Amaury.

Rawlin took them to a café to have a coffee and look at them. He had no idea how emotional he would get whenever he looked at them. He had to leave the café. He got so upset. How could he have let Amaury go? He'd been an idiot! He simply had to find him before his plane left at 1:05 pm the following day, even if he had to stay up all night to do it.

Meanwhile, Amaury was once again on the streets. Despite the rest and a dry bed at Charles and Syril's place, he was not feeling himself. His stomach and head were hurting, so he bought a Sprite and sat on a bench to drink it. Even it did not sit well today.

Whenever Amaury threw up blood again, he was scared. He didn't know what to do. He was not going back to Rawlin. Instead, he just roamed the streets until it was late at night. The next time he threw up, there was a lot of blood, and his head began to spin. He had to get some help. Something was seriously wrong with him.

He went to the clinic, but it was dark inside. He banged and banged on the door, but no one came. He was about to give up when he saw the light come on in the hallway. He began to bang again, yelling that he needed help, this time. A nurse came to the door to tell him that they were closed for the day.

"I came here before, and you sent me to the hospital. I was supposed to come back, but I didn't. I am throwing up more blood this time. Please help me."

The world began to spin again, and he felt the nurse steady him as she led him inside the clinic.

"Is your name Amaury?" She sat him down in a chair. "We've been hoping you'd come back. Why didn't you?"

"I started to feel better, so I decided I didn't need to come back. Now, there's blood again, and it scared me."

"You need to go to the hospital, Amaury. Your tests showed that you needed to be admitted. I think I'll drive you over there myself and ring the doctor on the way." She helped Amaury to his feet and out the back door to her car.

The hospital was not far, and she made the phone call to the clinic doctor, who said he would meet them at the hospital.

Parking at the Urgencies Entrance, the attendants helped him inside, leading him to an examining room. A nurse helped him onto the table, where he could lay down. Amaury had to close his eyes to stop the world from turning. The nurse began to talk to him.

"I need to ask you some questions. What's your full name, age, and address?" As sick as he was, Amaury didn't think. He just answered the questions this time. He just didn't care anymore.

"Amaury Rousseau, I'm nineteen, no, twenty, and I have no address but Paris."

"You live on the streets?" Amaury nodded. "The clinic nurse said that you were throwing up blood? Is it in your urine and bowels, as well?"

"No, not when I pee or anything. I threw up blood about a half-hour ago, I think. Twice today, I do this. My head hurts so badly." The nurse wrote down the information. "Whom do we contact regarding your condition and to sign for you if you become unable to do it yourself, like a family member?" Amaury had no one. He couldn't bother his sister since she was pregnant. It might scare her enough to hurt her or the baby. "Surely there must be someone you want to be here with you, Amaury." He said nothing. There was no one.

The doctors had his test results quickly, giving him an IV for the pain, and soon, his eyes closed, and he fell asleep.

## Chapter 16

Rawlin was packing his last bag whenever the hotel phone rang. He sat on the bed and picked it up. "Rawlin Jones." It was the hotel's front desk.

"Mr. Jones, you have a call from the hospital regarding Amaury Rousseau. Would you like to take the call, or would you like for me to take a message?"

Rawlins's heart skipped a beat. Rousseau? So that was his last name.

"Put it through, immediately!" Rawlin stood and began to pace.

"Mr. Jones?" the attendant asked.

"Yes, this is he. What's wrong with Amaury?" He almost yelled at them.

"Amaury had your name and this hotel name written on a note in his pocket. He's been admitted to the hospital for treatment. Are you a family member?"

"No, I'm his……..he's with me….was with me….anyway, I'll be right there for him. What's wrong? Is he going to be okay?"

"Will you be responsible for him? We believe he has bleeding ulcers."

"Yes, yes, do whatever you need to do. Amaury's estranged from his family. Where are you located? I will be there as quickly as possible."

Rawlin ran down the stairs and out to the curb with the address. He managed to hail a taxi quickly and told the driver to head fast for the hotel. He would make it worth his while. He held up a $50 for the driver to see. The driver took off so fast it threw Rawlin against the backseat.

On the way, Rawlin tried to calm himself. They would treat him and let him go if it were only ulcers. It would be fine. Amaury was going to be okay.

Rawlin threw the money at the hospital to the driver, said 'thanks,' and ran into the hospital. He slid into the information desk, panting.

"I'm here for Amaury Rousseau. Can I see his doctor?" The nurse told him to have a seat, and they'd get his doctor. Rawlin couldn't sit! He paced back and forth in front of the desk until a doctor appeared. He was sweating by the time the man arrived.

"Mr. Jones, you are here for Amaury?" Rawlin could only nod. "He is resting quietly now. We are moving him into a room. Let's go over here and talk before you go see him." They walked over to the chairs. "Are you a relative?" Rawlin was getting tired of questions.

"Does it matter?" The doctor was patient with him and smiled.

"Somewhat, but not if he has no one else to care for him."

"I'm not family. Oh, hell, he's with me, okay? We're in a relationship." Rawlin didn't give a damn what this doctor thought of him as long as he helped Amaury.

"I understand. I'm glad you are here. I don't know if you are familiar with the French health system, but it will pay for most of Amaury's needs. Will you be responsible for decisions and other expenses not covered by the health system?"

"Yes, I'll pay the bill. You just give him the best treatment available. I'll sign whatever papers you need me to. Just tell me where to sign."

"You can take care of that after you see him for a moment. He has bleeding ulcers. He went to our clinic before, and they sent him for tests. He never went back to the clinic for a follow-up." He has an intra-abdominal abscess, we believe. I was just about to get the results of the x-rays when you arrived."

"Okay, so how do you treat a bleeding ulcer? Does he need to stay in the hospital? For how long?" Rawlin shot questions at the doctor.

"Let's go see him. He was pretty scared when he came in. I'll answer your questions later."

The doctor took him down to one of the holding rooms and passed a couple of other beds before seeing Amaury. He was covered to the chest with a sheet and blanket, with an IV in his arm. The doctor told him it was a pain reliever. "Just stay with him for a few minutes, let him know you're here."

Rawlin nodded, and then the doctor left them alone. Rawlin walked to the bed, leaning over to take Amaury's hand. One of his tears fell and hit Amaury's face, waking him.

Amaury was in a fog, it seemed. He knew he was in the hospital and could see figures in white move about and work on him. Now he felt someone take his hand and something wet fell on his face. It was Rawlin. His heart leaped. He tried to talk but coughed instead, hurting his stomach.

"Don't try to talk, baby. The doctor said you have bleeding ulcers. They're going to take good care of you." But Amaury needed to talk.

Amaury tried again. His mouth was so dry it only came out as a garbled whisper. Rawlin stopped a nurse going past. "He's trying to talk, but his mouth is dry. Can he have a drink of water?" The nurse said that he could have ice and that she would bring some in a cup. Rawlin thanked her and returned to Amaury's side.

"I'm getting you some ice so your throat won't be so dry, baby. Just relax. I'm here for you. I'm here." Amaury sighed and closed his eyes again. How did Rawlin even know he was here? Why was he here? Shouldn't he have flown to Montreal by now? What day was it, anyway? Nothing made sense. Does he have ulcers?

Rawlin put the cup of ice to his lips, and Amaury ate a bite of it and then another. He could talk some now.

"Why are you here, Rawlin?" Rawlin wiped his face and leaned over to kiss Amaury's cheek.

"Because this is where I want to be, baby. I'm going to make sure they treat you right." Amaury was still confused, but he was too tired to talk anymore.

He closed his eyes and let himself drift again. "Amaury, I have to let you sleep now. I'll take care of the paperwork and talk to the doctor again, okay? Just rest now, Amaury." Amaury opened his eyes to see Rawlin walking away, and then he slept again.

Rawlin went to the waiting room next to the information desk to wait for news of Amaury. The nurse had him fill out some financial forms while he waited. "I can't fill a lot of this stuff in because he doesn't have an address or family here. Shall I just put my address in the states?" She said that he could.

At least he knew Amaury's full name now. The rest of the information was his own, back in Lubbock. He filled in what he could and then handed the forms back to the nurse. He would have to wait another 45 minutes before seeing the doctor again. The man sat next to him.

"We are sure that he has an intra-abdominal abscess now. We are giving him an IV of antibiotics right now. We will need to drain the abscess with a needle through the skin. We will drain the fluid build-up in it and leave the drain in so that it can drain the fluid out until the abscess goes away."

"How long will that take?"

"Usually a few days or a week, depending upon how bad it is. This one looks small on the x-ray. I think that perhaps a week should be enough. Then we will remove the drain whenever the infection goes away."

"I see. And then what treatment is there afterward?"

"I'll give him another round of oral antibiotics, and he'll need to be on a special diet for a while until the stomach has had time to heal. We'll give you a copy of that."

"Do you have to do surgery to insert the drain?"

"Just a local anesthetic will be used. Amaury should be able to go home in a couple of days." Good news for Rawlin. He could rent the apartment, set things up, and have someone pick Amaury up and drive him to the new place. After that, all he'd have to do was hire a cook to fix the special diet for Amaury. He felt better now. He could look Amaury in the eye and go to his job in Montreal.

"Thank you, doctor. I'll make sure that he has the right foods to eat. I'll be having a driver pick him up whenever he's released. I'm going to rent an apartment for him. I'll leave the company's name to pick him up with the Nurses. They have all of my financial information. I gave them my cell phone number here and back in the states."

"That's fine, Mr. Jones. We'll be moving Amaury into room 118 later. At seven in the morning, we will do the surgery. He should be back in his room in a couple of hours."

"Great! My flight leaves after one tomorrow. The timing will work out perfectly for me. I will be here as soon as I get the apartment taken care of and check out of my hotel." The two men shook hands. "Can I stay in the room with him tonight?"

"If you wish to sleep in the chair, you may. We have no beds for you."

"That's fine."

Rawlin waited until a nurse told him that Amaury was asleep in his new room. Only then did Rawlin go into the room, where he found a blanket and pillow in the chair. He thanked the nurse and then sat down, took off his boots, and got settled for the remainder of the night. It was already almost one o'clock now. He would need to be up early to do what he needed to do before leaving for the airport. Rawlin would fall asleep very quickly.

## Chapter 17

Amaury walked toward the train station, and after arguing with an employee about his not wearing a shirt or shoes, he managed to get on a train. He got off at Challis and sat on a bench near the platform and the tracks. He stared at them for a long time. Had Arnaud sat here contemplating suicide before he'd jumped? Or had he just done it without thinking? It was where Arnaud had died at sixteen young years old. And now, here he was, barely twenty, thinking of doing the same thing. A raindrop fell onto his face, followed by more and more. Amaury looked up at the gloomy sky, and as he did, an angry voice said,

"Move along." He looked up into the face of a policeman. When Amaury didn't say or do anything, the officer had nudged his shoulder roughly. "Go on, get out of here, boy." Amaury stood, hugged his naked torso, and walked away. He just needed to get back to his locker to get a shirt and jacket. Then he could be warm. He just went around the corner, waited until the policeman was gone, and then boarded a train.

Amaury sat in a corner cowering, a coward who couldn't jump. It would have been over now if he'd been brave. Now he was just so sad that he felt empty.

Some of the passengers gave him disapproving or curious looks. He wouldn't meet their eyes. It was none of their business what his story was.

Amaury pulled out a brown shirt at his locker, and then he noticed that the jacket wasn't there. Damn it! He'd left it in the hotel room, along with his only pair of shoes. He pulled on the shirt and sat on one of the benches to think. It was still raining. He had to get somewhere warm to rest and decide what to do. He would go to Jean-Marc.

Amaury took the train to the aunt's house where Jean-Marc lived now. It was pouring down rain, now. Amaury knocked on the door. The aunt herself answered the door. He'd hoped it would be Jean-Marc.

"May I see Jean-Marc? I am a friend of his. I need to talk to him." She looked down at his bare feet and wet condition and frowned. Jean-Marc came to the door shortly after that.

A cow boy in Paris

"Amaury, what are you doing here?" The boy looked down at his feet.

"May I just stay here with you until the rain goes away, and I can dry out? I've lost my shoes and jacket, and I am so wet." Jean-Marc looked at him with pity. Amaury could just imagine what he looked like to others.

"I can't, Amaury. My aunt will not allow you into the house. She knows about your last visit and that you hustle. She said to send you away. I'm sorry."

"That's okay, Jean-Marc. I don't wish to get you into any trouble. I will go and manage. I always do because I must."

"Amaury, wait here for a moment." Jean-Marc went back into the house while Amaury stood there in the drenching rain. He came back a few moments later. "Take these, please. It's the least I can do for you, Amaury." Jean-Marc's aunt yelled at him to shut the door. "I'm so sorry, Cheri. I must go. You take care."

And he closed the door. Amaury pulled the red sweater over his head. It was too big, but it was warm. Then he knelt to put on the black lace-up shoes. They looked like something an older man would wear to a funeral, but at least they would protect his feet. Amaury was grateful.

He began to hurry toward the train station. As he went, it didn't take long for the sweater to become just as drenched as his brown shirt had been. He rode out to an area where he knew Rawlin wouldn't find him. He needed to work and make some money, so he cruised the place for about an hour before finding someone interested. The man pulled him roughly into one of the stalls, and after he got what he wanted from Amaury, he threw some money on the floor and left him there. Many men treated him this way. He was used to it, but it made him feel less than human today. These men just wanted to use you and then throw you away until an urge rose in them the next time.

Amaury bent down to put the money in his shoe. They had begun to rub blisters on his bare skin. He stuck the money and then some toilet tissue into the back edge to prevent further damage. It didn't help. Soon, it was getting hard to walk, and the blisters had burst, and both feet were bleeding. He just had to get some socks. He needed more money. But the rain had finally quit, so everyone was back onto the streets, and very few men were in the station, looking. Amaury decided to return to his old ways and steal some socks. He couldn't use the money he'd just earned. It was all he had, and what if an emergency came up?

He took another train to an area with a department store. He found some thick black socks, hid them in his jeans, and then headed out to the sidewalk. He only made it a few feet when a security guard stopped him. Amaury tried to get away, but it was no use. The man was too strong, and he, too weak, and his feet were killing him.

The security guard pulled him into the back office and ordered him to sit.

"Name?" the guard asked, but Amaury said nothing. "It would be in your best interest to cooperate, kid. What is your name?"

"Napoleon Bonaparte." The man was getting angry now.

"Do you have your ID?" Amaury said he didn't have one. The man's voice became louder. "The Police will throw your nameless little ass in the jail, and I won't have to deal with you any longer!" He began to write something on the form just as another man poked his head into the office.

"Louis, how are you? I haven't been by here in a while." Amaury noted that the man was good-looking. He smiled at Amaury. Bad cop, good cop, routine? Perhaps. "So, what's going on with this one?" The guard held up the pair of socks." The man at the door broke into a grin. Louis didn't think it was funny at all. "I'm sorry, Louis, but is that all he took?" The guard began to say that a crime was and should know that. "Yes, I know, Louis. Hey, I'll take care of this one, okay? Thank you for a job well done." The guard gave Amaury a nasty look, and then he walked out of the room. This new man sat in his place. He handed the socks to Amaury. "I'm Detective Monet. You know, like the painter? What is your name?"

"Amaury." He was so tired and cold.

"The last name, please?" Amaury told him that he did not have a last name anymore. The man nodded. "You are on the streets, then?" Amaury nodded. Somehow, he sensed this man was genuine.

"My family disowned me long ago, so I am just Amaury."

"Well, Amaury, I understand your situation. Do you steal to get by?"

"No, not anymore. I did long ago, but you see, it's my feet. They bleed, and I am hurting and have to do something, so I decided to steal what I needed."

The detective looked down at his feet, pulling up one then the other of his pant legs. He winced at what he saw. He called the floor of the store for the guard, who returned.

"Did you see this boy's bloody feet?" Louis looked and shook his head. "Get the First Aid kit, will you, please." The detective then tore up the theft report. "The socks are on me. Let's get you bandaged up, and then perhaps we can find a decent pair of shoes in your size. What do you say?" Amaury was very suspicious.

The guard returned with the kit and left in a huff whenever he saw the torn theft form in the trash container. "Are you positive?" he asked. Amaury just looked at him. "Are you HIV positive, or do you have AIDS?" Amaury shook his head. "Have you ever been arrested before?" Again, Amaury shook his head as the man put one foot up on the desk, bandaging it, and then the other one. "There you go." Amaury put his leg back on the floor. "Put those socks on, please. What size shoe do you wear?" Amaury told him. "If you promise to stay here while I find you some shoes, I will not file the charges of theft. Will you stay?"

Yes, he would.

Amaury waited for the detective to return with some shoes. It was very weird, but as he'd felt before, this man was trustworthy.

The detective returned with a couple of pairs of shoes not long after. Amaury carefully tried both sets, liking the black ankle boots zipped up.

"Stand up and walk. Make sure these boots don't rub anywhere."

Amaury stood slowly and walked a few steps. They felt pretty good, except for the blistered spots, which still ached.

"They are fine." Amaury sat back down. The detective saw the money stuck into the old shoes. He got it out, holding it up to Amaury. "I can't spend that money. It is all I have, and I might need it for more important things."

The detective laughed, shaking his head. He handed Amaury the money. "No, you take it for the socks and shoes. I will pay back the rest as soon as I can."

"I'm sure that you would, but I won't let you. As you said, you might need this for more important things than socks. Put it in your new shoe." Amaury did.

"Come on. Let's get out of here. I am just off duty now." The funeral shoes went into the trash on the way out of the store. "Why don't you come and get your clothes dry at my place." Amaury shook his head.

"You do enough for me, already. Merci." He held out his hand. The man smiled and put a hand on his shoulder.

"I was like you once, Amaury. I was kicked out of my home and hustled on the streets. Then I met someone who helped me, and then he loved me. I changed. I decided that I wanted to be a policeman and help people like myself."

"You are gay? I didn't see it. I'm usually very precise on the subject."

The detective laughed again. It was a nice, warm laugh.

"I hide it well. It wouldn't do my career any good if my department knew about my partner and me. Amaury knew it was true. He's a policeman too."

"So, will you come and let us at least get you dry, warm, and fed? My car is just over here." Amaury went with the Detective to his car. The apartment was not far away. The man let him lean on him as they walked into the street-level apartment. "Syril! Honey, are you home?" A voice answered from the kitchen, so they walked that way. A tall, handsome man was there, making fresh coffee.

"Who have you brought home this time, sweetheart? He's so wet!"

"Yes, he is. This young man is Amaury, and we're going to get his clothes dry, get him some sleep and warmth, and feed him." The man had a deep voice.

"How about a hot bath, Cheri? I can wash and dry your clothes while you soak and get warm."

"That would be great, yes." The two men exchanged looks and nods.

"Charles, you take him to the tub and get those clothes to me, love." He kissed the detective, and then Charles led him down the hall.

"Let me get the water running, and then you can get out of those wet clothes. You can just put them outside the door if you want privacy." But Amaury had already pulled the sweater and his shirt off in one swoop and was unbuttoning his pants by the time the word 'privacy' came out.

Charles just laughed and went about getting Amaury a towel and even adding bubbles to the bath. "Your feet will sting whenever the hot water hits them, but then they will feel better." Charles gathered up the clothes. "Enjoy the bath as long as you want. We'll be in the kitchen making dinner when you get out."

Left alone, Amaury stepped into the water. He'd decided to leave the bandages on at first, thinking it wouldn't hurt as much. It did hurt, though, and he pulled off the applications and then got into the water again. It didn't take long before the pain eased, and his whole body began to feel better. He slid down to let his head go under the water a couple of times, too. It felt heavenly.

After he dried off, Amaury found a blue robe hanging on the outside of the door. He slipped it on and walked down to the kitchen. Soft music filled the air and the aroma of food that smelled wonderful to Amaury, who was starving. Before they saw him, he stood in the hallway watching the two lovers for a few moments. They were cooking together, sipping wine, all the while, talking about their day, including him.

"Ah, he's out of the tub," Syril said as he turned to find Amaury watching them. "Come on in, sweetheart, and have a seat." Amaury walked to the table and sat at one of the chairs. Charles came over to him with a box of bandages and tape. "Let's see these blisters that Charlie told me about." Charles picked up one of his feet as Syril looked on. "Oh, Cheri, that's terrible. You poor thing!"

Charles re-bandaged his feet, and then Amaury volunteered to help them.

"Is there anything I can do to help? I can't cook, but perhaps there's something else I could do to help repay your kindness."

"Nonsense! You are our guest! Just relax and enjoy our home and food. Your clothes should be dry soon, too. And you can get some sleep tonight, too."

Amaury wouldn't stay the night. That would be too much. He appreciated these two for helping him, but he would never get close to anyone again.

The three of them sat down to eat some rice and vegetables and lamb, and the men talked about their life with him.

Amaury ate a plateful of food and was getting very sleepy. His clothes were now dry, so he put them back on and the new socks before lying on the couch to get a nap. When Syril went to get him a blanket, Amaury asked Charles about the two of them.

"Syril is older than you, isn't he?" Charles gathered a couple of pillows, sticking them under Amaury's head.

"Yes, he is eleven years older than me. Why do you ask?" Amaury was curious about their relationship.

"Did he pick you up and then stay with you?" Charles nodded. "How long?"

"Well, I was seventeen whenever we met, and he was twenty-eight. I'm forty-one, now. It works for us. I love him very much." Syril had returned with the blanket, and Charles blew him a kiss. "And he loves me, very much, too."

"Yes, I do!" Syril laid the blanket over Amaury, whose eyes were heavy. The last thing he remembered was Charles sitting in the rocker with a newspaper while Syril sat in a wing chair with a book. He let himself drift off. Despite what he'd said about not staying the night, he ended up staying two.

## Chapter 18

The nurses came in at six o'clock to get Amaury ready for his procedure. Rawlin needed to get up anyway, to get out of the way.

"Hi, baby. They need to put you to sleep to drain that ulcer of yours. You'll be back in the room in about two hours. I'll be here when you wake up." He kissed Amaury on the lips. Amaury opened his eyes. Rawlin had kissed him with people in the room. Wow! He felt so oddly. He wanted to say something to Rawlin, but he just didn't have the energy to do so. He smiled and closed his eyes again.

Rawlin went by the hotel, finished packing the bags, and left them down in the lobby so he could get to the airport faster.

After grabbing some coffee and a croissant, Rawlin caught a taxi to the area where he'd noticed a quaint apartment building earlier, and the idea had come to him to get an apartment for Amaury.

George called him while signing the six-month lease for the furnished apartment. Yes, he would be on the flight to Montreal today, he told him.

Amaury made it through the procedure without any problems. The doctor met Rawlin at the nurse's station whenever he returned. He had found a second ulcer, more minor, but he had also taken care of it. Everything looked good.

"Thank you so much, doc. Is he sleeping?"

"He's coming in and out of the anesthetic. He's feeling no pain now, that's for sure." The doctor smiled, patted him on the back, and headed on his way.

Amaury felt someone pick up his arm. He looked down to see a pretty nurse sticking another IV into his arm. She smiled at him.

"Ah, you are awake. I am giving you some more pain medication to rest well. I will put a cup of ice here, in case you want to wet your mouth later." Amaury just blinked his eyes at her. She was leaving the room when Rawlin came in.

"Hi, baby. I'm glad you're awake." He kissed his lips. "Your procedure went great. You have a drain for the ulcers. It has to stay there until all of that fluid drains, and then they'll take out the tube later." Amaury looked down to see the tube. He couldn't. Right then, he didn't care.

Rawlin pulled up a chair and sat beside him, feeding him some ice chips, which helped a lot.

"What day is this?" He needed to know why Rawlin was still here.

"It's Friday morning." Rawlin took his hand. "I have been looking for you everywhere that I could think of, but it was like you disappeared. I was so upset."

"How did you know I was here? I didn't tell them to call you." He started to cough, so Rawlin gave him more ice chips. "I am not your responsibility."

"You had my name and the hotel number on a note in your pocket. The hospital found it and rang me. I came as fast as I could."

Now it made sense. Amaury had had some rough clients lately, so he decided that if his body was found injured or dead, they could at least have Rawlin take care of or bury him if things got out of control. He hadn't expected this.

"I have a wonderful surprise for you tomorrow. I've rented an apartment with a view of the Eifel Tower. It's got three rooms and is quaint and romantic, and I know you will love it! It's the Paris Auteuil Apartments, number 628."

Amaury was stunned. Did Rawlin just say that he'd rented them an apartment? He prayed he understood correctly. "Now you know that I have to go to Montreal today, Amaury. I simply cannot get out of it without quitting my job." Amaury was even more confused. "I have to leave for the airport in a few minutes. I will be back here as soon as I can be. I'm just so happy that I found you and that you will be okay." He gave Amaury another kiss. "I'm going to send your things here, to the hospital, so that you can take them to the new apartment. I'm going over there to get my bags now." He gently hugged Amaury. "I hate to leave you here in this hospital bed, but I have to go. I'll come to get

## A cow boy in Paris

you as soon as I can. How about a Texas Christmas?"

One more kiss, and Amaury watched the man he loved walk out the door. He hadn't said anything because he was afraid he had been dreaming.

## Chapter 19

The plane set down in Montreal. Rawlin made his way off the plane, heading for Baggage Claim. He got a cart, loaded it, and then went to rent a truck for the job site. He called George, who gave him directions to the location. He found Duncan, the foremen, in the company trailer when he got there.

"Hey, Rawlin Jones, the missing man." He stood up to shake Rawlins's hand.

"I thought I'd never get over here, man. I'm glad to hear that things are going well."

"Yes, it should be a week or so, and we should finish, Jones. Glad you could come over to help us out."

Rawlin headed out to the truck and drove to the hotel. It was late by the time he got there. It was almost eight o'clock. He wanted to call Amaury, but he didn't want to wake him up, so he didn't. He would just have to place a call at seven o'clock, Paris time, at work. Then he'd have to call his family in Texas. He was not looking forward to it. There were too many ghosts in Texas.

A cow boy in Paris

And how the hell was he going to explain Amaury to them? He'd figure that out when he had to.

## Chapter 20

Amaury had slept through the night thanks to the medicine. It was the ringing of the telephone that woke him. A nurse answered it and then handed the phone to him. He spoke in a whisper, "Salut?"

"Hi, baby, it's me. I knew I'd wake you, but I promised to call you."

Amaury cleared his throat and began to speak in French very quickly as he remembered what was going on. Rawlin had to stop him. "Hey, too fast! Slower and in English, please, baby."

Amaury forgot himself, tried to move too fast into a more comfortable position, and yelled out in pain. He dropped the phone in the process. "Amaury? Amaury! Get a nurse!" Rawlin could only wait. He felt so helpless. The nurse who'd answered the phone helped Amaury sit up and handed him the receiver.

"I am here, cowboy. So sorry. I hurt myself, and I dropped the phone."

"What? Is the nurse there to help you?" Amaury told him what had happened.

"Are you okay now? Did they get you something for pain?"

"Oui, Oui, I am just very sore, Cheri. I have to be careful."

"I wish I was there for you. I'm so sorry that I can't be."

Amaury didn't say anything, so Rawlin brought up the apartment.

"I can't wait for you to see the apartment, baby. It's perfect, and the view is something I think you'll enjoy." Amaury let out a deep breath he'd been holding. He wasn't going to bring up the subject, afraid that he'd just dreamed about this happening. Rawlin had leased them an apartment.

"They say I leave the hospital tomorrow if things look well. This is good news."

Yes, it was great news.

"I told you that I hired a driver to take you to the apartment from the hospital. Do you remember?" Amaury did. "Do you see the bags with your things in them? They should be there for you to take to the apartment." Amaury saw the bags next to the chair by the door.

"Oui, they are here."

"Good. I've arranged to have your meals cooked for you. A lady that lives in the same apartment building will be contacting you about it, okay?" Amaury was frowning.

"What special foods? Bland? Pooh!" Rawlin laughed at him a little.

"If bland means mild to you, then yes, they'll be bland. You can't just go back to eating anything, or it will hurt your stomach."

Amaury needed to know something, but he was afraid to ask. It turns out he didn't have to. Rawlins's next question answered it for him. "Do you have a passport? I sure hope so, or this could become complicated." A passport must mean that Rawlin did plan to take him to Texas for Christmas, as he'd said.

"Oui, I have a passport. At least I did have a passport when I lived at the vineyard. It's still there unless they threw it away with me." Rawlin sure hoped not. If Amaury had to apply for a new passport, it would take time. He didn't know how long, but the holidays would have come and gone by the time he got a new one. "Rawlin?" Amaury was getting nervous when he didn't say anything.

"Huh? Oh, just thinking. Can you find out quickly? Your sister would know, wouldn't she? She could get it to you. Can you call her today? Time is of the essence."

Amaury would have to call his former home. His sister and her husband still lived on the property. He didn't want to call the vineyard, but he'd do it if it meant spending Christmas in Texas with Rawlin.

"Oui, I can call her if they'll let me place a call from the hospital."

"Just tell them to put it on the bill. I'll take care of it. And if you don't have one anymore, we'll need your birth certificate so we can apply for a new one."

That would mean that he wouldn't go to Texas for Christmas. Amaury knew it would take too long, and he said so. "We'll just hope that it's still there and if it's not, take it from there." Amaury knew it was all that he could do. "I will call you again soon, to find out how you like the apartment and if you have the passport. I left the cell phone that I was using over there at the apartment for you to use."

"That would be nice, to have a phone. Merci, Cheri." Amaury had a change of heart regarding the phone.

"You can call who you want. I don't mind." Rawlin felt a little deceptive saying this. He had an ulterior motive. He could see who Amaury called. Now maybe the boy's life would become less of a mystery. "I'm gonna let you go, baby. It would be best if you rested, and so do I. I just got off work, and it was a long day."

Amaury was exhausted already from the surgery. "I'll call you soon. Hopefully, you can give me good news about the passport."

"Okay. I am looking so forward to seeing our new place, Cheri." Rawlin could already hear his breathing getting heavier and more even.

"I love you, sweetie. I'll talk to you soon."

"I love you too." Amaury hung up the phone and his eyes closed as the phone hit the bed. He was asleep.

Rawlin got undressed and into bed. He couldn't get one thing Amaury had said out of his head. He'd said 'OUR' new place. Yes, Rawlin was sure he'd said it. He turned off the lamp and fell asleep.

## Chapter 21

Up early the following day, Rawlin figured he might as well give his parents a call. They'd be up early. They'd been living on the farm or ranch for all of these years. He poured himself a cup of black coffee, sat in the chair in his room, and dialed the number. It only rang twice before his mother picked up.

"Rawlin! My baby! I've been waiting for you to call, honey."

"Hi, Mom. I figured I'd better call to let you know that I'm on this side of the pond before you sic George on me again." She laughed.

"It's true! We've had him after you for a while now." She laughed again. "Enough of that for now. How is my baby boy? Tell me the truth, Rawlin Jones. I'm your Mother. I'll know if you are." Rawlin took a drink of the coffee.

"I'm fine, Mom. I wish all of you would stop worrying about me so much. I work and work because I like to work." She corrected him.

"You like to work because it keeps your mind busy, and you don't have any time to think about your personal life." That was true. At least it had been before he met Amaury. She went on. "Is it true that you are coming home for the holidays?" What had George told them, anyway?

"Just for Christmas, Mom. We'll just have to see after that. I have a job in Europe coming up soon, so...." She was talking to him already.

"Rawlin, why do you have to work so far away from home? Why can't you just work in the states, son? We miss you so much. And Candy could use your support right now." Rawlin took another drink. He just could not tell her that wasn't going to happen. Then he realized what she'd said at the end.

"What's going on with Candy?" His sister was a tough cookie. Why did she need him? "How old are her kids now, anyway?"

"She and Butch are getting a divorce, Rawlin. They've separated, so we knew it was coming, but it's a terrible thing. He wouldn't go for counseling."

Rawlin hated to hear it. He had just assumed that Candy could handle whatever life gave her. She always had.

"What went wrong, Mom? How are the kids taking it?"

His mother told him that they'd been growing apart, separated, and then Butch had gotten himself a girlfriend.

"A girlfriend?" He chuckled. "And he's still alive?"

"It's not funny, Rawlin. " Rawlin apologized, explaining that he just figured that Candy would have killed him whenever she found out about the other woman. "And those kids are acting out something terrible over it. They're giving Candy hell, Rawlin, and Butch. He won't help her at all."

"How old are those kids now, anyway? Aren't they in high school?"

"You've been away too long, son. Josie is twenty, a sophomore at Northwest Texas State, and Linus is 17 and a Junior in high school." Damn! He was out of touch. "They were always so well-behaved before

A cowboy in Paris

this, Rawlin. Linus could use a man in his life." Rawlin sighed

"I can't believe those kids are that old. But Candy is thirty-eight, right?"

"That's right. She sure is, but don't remind your sister. She feels like she's fifty." I'll give her a call as soon as I can, Mom. I don't know how much help I can be, but I can sure try." They agreed this was a good idea. It seemed as if the kids were acting out because they didn't know what else to do, and Candy was there to take the brunt of it all. Now Rawlin had to bring up the subject that he'd been avoiding. He'd just act as if it were no big deal.

"The plan is that I'll get down to Lubbockon the eighteenth and come to Abernathy on the 20th. "It will be the traditional family Christmas week." He took a deep breath and just said it. "Um, would it be alright if I bring someone with me?" Rawlin's mom laughed out loud, with glee.

"Oh, son, that would be so wonderful! Of course, you can. Why didn't you mention that you'd met someone to us? We've all wanted this so badly. George said that you'd met someone in France."

"Mom, don't make a big deal out of this." If she only knew that he was talking about a man. What would she say? He decided to end the call before she asked him anything else. "Mom, I've gotta get to work. I'll talk to you soon." He hung up with her still talking, and took a big drink of the coffee. It was cold now. He got up and poured it down the drain, got ready for work, and then headed that way.

## Chapter 22

Amaury asked the nurse to make a phone call to Reins, adding it to his bill. They said that he could, so he picked up the phone. He still knew the number by memory, so he took a deep breath and gave the nurse the number.

Amalie had moved into the guest house after she had married. His brother-in-law answered.

"Loren, It's Amaury. Is my sister available?"

"Amaury? What a surprise. Amalie is with her mother. They shop for baby things. She is not here. Can I help?" Amaury knew he could count on Loren.

"Oui. I need my passport. It would be with the others if they kept it at all. Do you know where it would be?" Loren said that he had seen Amaury's passport in the fire safe whenever he had recently put some essential papers into the safe. "Could Amalie bring it to me later this week? I need it as soon as possible, Loren."

"Can't you simply come to get it, Amaury?" The thought of going back there made his heart begin to beat faster. He just couldn't do it.

"Loren, please understand. I cannot go back there. I just can't!"

"Amaury, I don't want Amalie to ride the train in her condition. She is very fragile. The doctor says that she is delicate in this pregnancy." Amaury began to get worried. Could she lose the baby?

"Is she okay? Is the baby going to be okay?" Please let nothing be wrong.

"She just needs to be careful. She had two miscarriages before, Amaury. She doesn't tell you because she didn't want to worry you."

"I'm so sorry, Loren. She needs to stay home. I understand, Loren. Could you possibly bring it to me? I hate to ask you, but I have an opportunity to travel to the United States for Christmas."

"I can bring it to Paris for you if it means this much to you. In two days, I can come in on the train if that is working for you." Amaury was again relieved.

"That would be perfect. I will meet you at the train station in two days. Take the train that arrives at 1:30." Loren agreed that he would do it.

"Loren, please don't let anyone know what you are doing. They might not let you have the passport if they know." Loren said that he would be careful.

After he got off the phone with Loren, Amaury could rest now and look forward to moving into their new apartment and going to Texas for Christmas with Rawlin.

He imagined he and Rawlin curled up on the couch together on a cold Paris night, safe and warm in their place. They'd be in love and share their lives. He fell asleep thinking about his future with the cowboy.

## Chapter 23

After a day's work, Rawlin headed back to the hotel. He took a shower, put on some pajama pants, ordered a pizza, and sat down to phone his sister to find out how things were going. Maybe he could help her with the kids and the divorce situation. He didn't even know what to say to teenagers, but he'd try.

The phone rang and went to voicemail. Rawlin left a message whenever his older sister picked up the phone out of breath.

"Rawlin, hey! It's so good to hear your voice. How are you doing?"

"I'm working. You know me. Things are looking up, sis. I guess I'm going to be seeing you guys at Christmas." She was happy about this.

"That's what I hear. I talked to mom after you called her. She is over the moon that you're back. So am I. And my kids are all excited about seeing their famous Uncle Rawlin, world traveler, again." Rawlin groaned.

"Is Mom that bad about making me larger than life?" His sister said that both of their parents talked about him all the time. "I'm so sorry that you have to go through all of that over me. I hope I'm not a big disappointment to all of you."

"That will never happen, Rawlin." Rawlin wondered what she'd think of his being gay. He had no idea how she'd react. He steered the conversation back to her.

"Mom told me about you and Butch. I was sorry to hear about that. And she said the kids weren't taking it so well either." She sighed loudly.

"Well, I'm not sorry about it. Rawlin. He was always a selfish jerk who expected me to wait on him hand and foot and never question his authority."

Rawlin had to admit that he'd never really warmed up to Butch much. Candy had only seen him a short time whenever she became pregnant with Josie.

"Why did you stay with him so long, then? I never thought he treated you like he should have." She laughed at this comment.

"He expected me to be his perfect little wife, who was seen, not heard. I stayed for the kid's sake, I guess. And whenever Josie left home, I got so depressed that I started overeating. I weigh 287 pounds, Rawlin." That was hard for him to imagine. Now Candy had been about 30 pounds overweight, but 287 but a lot of extra weight.

"He started calling me names because of the weight and when I wouldn't wait on him any longer or keep a perfect house." Her voice was cracking. "And the kids heard it, and that made me feel so low. I just ate more." Rawlin could just hear Butch calling her fat or lazy. He was way too blunt. But Candy had always been so challenging. She was too tough on people sometimes. She'd been through mean and nice periods as they'd grown up together. "And then he went and got that skank of a girlfriend. She's thin as a rail and plain, but still, couldn't he at least wait until we were officially divorced?"

"Do the kids blame you, or are they just upset about the whole thing?"

"Oh, I don't know. I guess the kids think I drove their dad away by letting myself go and not keeping him happy at home or something. I always let Butch discipline the kids, and they don't listen to me, Rawlin. They just won't mind me."

"Aren't you paying for Josie's school, and probably a truck for Linus, if I'm guessing right? You have great leverage, Candy, if you use it to your advantage." It sounded lame when he said it out loud.

"Yes, on both accounts. I can use it as a last resort, I guess. But I hate to hold things over their head like that. What if they just say, 'I don't care or something? They're just making some bad choices, Rawlin. I don't know."

"What kinds of choices? What are they doing? Maybe I could talk to them."

"Could you? That would be just wonderful! They both admire you, especially Linus." Candy told him that Josie was dating a thirty-six-year-old man, and Linus was hanging out with this new kid at school that his mom did not like.

"What's wrong with him? Is he a gang-banger or something?" She burst out laughing.

"Quite the contrary, little brother! He's more feminine than I am, I swear. Do you know what I mean? And he and Linus are inseparable! It scares me, Rawlin."

A sick feeling came over Rawlin. He didn't say anything. "I just don't like it."

He decided to change the subject.

"So, Josie is a sophomore at Northwestern? She's still attending classes, right?" Candy said that's she'd been skipping class to see this man she'd mentioned. "Just tell her how important an education will be to her."

"She throws that one back in my face since I didn't go to college. I was hoping that you'd come in handy there."

"Yes, I can talk to them about education, Candy, and anything else you want me to. What does Josie want to major in?"

"She wants to be a dentist. I just hope she doesn't end up pregnant like I did before I was ready with her. It was so tough".

To Rawlin, it sounded as if the kids were just unsure of what would happen and who would be there for them. He asked if Butch was still seeing them at all. No, he was too busy with his new girlfriend.

"Linus won't even talk to him anymore because he just grips about me, to him." She was getting emotional again. "He's pretty sensitive, Rawlin. I worry about how naïve he is." Was it possible that his nephew was gay like he was? He hoped not, for the boy's sake. It was too hard. "He won't talk to me about how he feels anymore."

It was she who changed the subject now to his life.

"So, who are you bringing with you? Mom was so happy whenever you asked if you could bring someone to the farm. She's always worried about you ending up alone. We all do." He was sure hoping she wouldn't ask him this.

"Mom worries about me too much. You all do. I'm a big boy. I can manage."

"You're trying to change the subject. Who are you bringing?"

He couldn't just say it like that. He hadn't thought about how he would even introduce Amaury to his family.

"I'm bringing a friend for Christmas, yes, from France."

"A friend from France. Hmmm, that's interesting." She laughed.

"A friend. Yes, I do have a friend or two, Candy." He had to get off the phone. The pizza saved his ass. "Look, gotta go. My pizza is here, and I am starving. I'll talk to you soon."

"It is so good to hear from you, and I can't wait to see you, Rawlin."

"Me too, Candy. I'll see you soon."

Rawlin hung up, satisfied, for now, anyway, paid for his pizza, ate, and then got into bed and tried to sleep. He gave up after an hour of just lying there.

Rawlin got a drink of water. He wondered how Amaury was doing and hoped he wasn't in too much pain.

Rawlin felt better knowing that Amaury would be safer now. Memories of their time

### A cow boy in Paris

together and touring the city helped. It made him smile, and his mind slowed down a little.

Finally, Rawlin got back into bed, and this time, he was able to sleep.

## Chapter 24

The nurses woke Amaury early, telling him that the doctor would be by soon to look him over and discuss what he needed to do, and then he would be released if everything looked good. He moved the bed into a sitting position and waited. Soon his breakfast arrived. He was eating the creamed wheat when the doctor came in.

"Good morning, Amaury. How are you feeling? It looks like you have an appetite. That's good. I just need to look at the drain and see what it looks like."

Amaury put his fork down so that the doctor could remove his bandages and look at the site of the drain. "You're going to be sore for a few days, Amaury. I have some pain pills for you to take home, and you'll have a special diet for a week at least. I gave a copy of the food list to Mr. Jones. He said he'd make sure you ate the proper food while you heal." Amaury nodded his head. "Nurse, re-bandage this, please. And Amaury, you can't take a shower until we remove the drain. It's sponge baths only, okay?"

"How long will the drain be in place?" The doctor told him that he'd return to the hospital in four days. If it has finished draining, then we can remove it. I think that will be enough." He shook Amaury's hand.

"You have someone picking you up, so you can go ahead and get dressed and ready to go. I'm off to complete my rounds. So take care of yourself, okay?" Amaury said that he would.

After getting dressed, all Amaury could do now was wait for the driver to get there. He was a little worried since he hadn't heard from Rawlin in a few days. He said that he'd call. Or had he? No, maybe he'd said he'd call whenever Amaury got to the apartment. Yes, that was it. He relaxed a little while he waited.

Another fifteen or twenty minutes passed before a nurse, and a man in a chauffer's suit came into the room. He held a driver's cap under his arm.

"Amaury, this man is here to drive you home. " She looked at the driver. "These are his things, here." The nurse came over for Amaury to sign the release papers, which he did. The driver picked up the bags and placed the hat back on his head.

"Are you ready to go home, sir?" Amaury nodded. He was beginning to get excited about the apartment now. Yes, he was going home.

The nurse walked Amaury out to the black car that waited in the drop-off area. The driver opened the door for Amaury, who carefully climbed inside. The man then sat the bags on the seat next to Amaury. Amaury thanked the nurse, the door closed, and the driver ran around getting inside the vehicle.

The first bump hurt Amaury's stomach, so he sat forward a bit, holding it as still as he could without hitting the drain.

As the streets of Paris passed by outside, Amaury felt as if he were watching someone else's life play out in a movie. He seemed to recall the address Rawlin had told him, but now he wasn't sure that was right. Which apartment would it be? Rawlin had good taste, so he wasn't worried too much. A smile came across his face, and he pinched himself to see if this was real, and it was.

The car rounded a corner stopping in front of the Paris Auteuil Apartments. Amaury had passed these apartments many times but never believed he'd be living here.

Butterflies flew in his stomach as he waited for the driver to come around to open his door. But, instead, he offered Amaury a hand. Amaury took it, feeling like a prince or someone special.

"I'll walk you inside and come back to get your things."

Amaury leaned on the man as they made their way inside, where he stopped to look around. It was perfect. Old-style charm lived in harmony with modern technology. They continued to the service desk, where an older woman curiously watched.

"I am to reside here. Mr. Rawlin Jones has secured us an apartment in the building. I am Amaury." She broke into a big smile, interrupting him.

"Amaury Rousseau. Yes, we have been expecting your arrival."

"Oui, I am Amaury." So Rawlin knew his name well now. Had he drawn the connection to the Rousseau Champagne? Did it matter anyway? He didn't care anymore. The woman handed him a key chain with two keys on it.

"The keys are to your door and your mailbox. You are number 628, Cheri. I just need for you to sign your lease right here," she pointed to a line, "and here." The driver, who had gone back out to get his things, put a hand on his shoulder.

"I'll be going now, sir. Enjoy your new apartment." Amaury shook the man's hand and thanked him for everything. Then he looked back at the paperwork. He scanned what he was about to sign. It all seemed very uniform, so he took the pen from the woman's hand, and then he stopped.

"Is everything paid for, or do I need to do anything regarding expenses?"

"Mr. Jones took care of the rental agreement for six months, sir. You don't owe a thing." Amaury signed the papers in both places. He noticed something that was either odd or very thoughtful of Rawlin. Nowhere on the lease was Rawlin's name. He decided not to worry about it. He'd ask Rawlin later.

A cow boy in Paris

The woman came around the desk, picking up the bags which the driver had sat in a chair. "I'll carry these for you. Mr. Jones said you were just out of the hospital, so you don't need to strain yourself." Amaury thanked her and followed across the lobby to the elevator, where they rode up to the sixth floor. She led him down the hall. "Unlock the door." He did, and then they walked inside.

Amaury was very impressed. All units had direct telephone lines, television with international cable channels, Wi-Fi broadband Internet access, and individual air conditioning. In addition, they had secretarial services, faxes, shopping services, delivery of meals, laundry, dry cleaning services, and laundry in the basement and baby-sitting. And in Amaury's unit, they had a double bed, storage cupboard, and desk, a window view of the street leading to a view of the Tower Eifel. So that was the view Rawlin had referred to. Amaury smiled at the thought of him.

The main room had a sofa and matching blue and yellow chair, a fireplace, a small dining table for two, and wooden floors with a large throw rug with blue and gold flowers.

"The kitchenette has a double hotplate, refrigerator, microwave oven, kettle, coffeemaker, crockery, glassware, cutlery, and kitchen utensils. It also has condiments and staples. Mr. Jones had us go shopping for these things for you."

Amaury opened the refrigerator door, looking inside. There were drinks, cheese, butter, ketchup, eggs, and other things that Rawlin knew he would like.

"Which way to the bedroom?" She pointed to a doorway near the desk. The room was small, so the double bed took up most space. It was an older wooden bed with a yellow and blue floral spread.

There were two nightstands on each side with lamps on them. And a couple of paintings on the wall of scenes of Paris.

They walked back into the main room.

"Mr. Jones has arranged to have your meals delivered to you for the week. He gave us a special diet for you to eat on. My sister lives in the building too. She will be cooking. She'll have a menu for you to choose from for dinner and your meals for tomorrow. Will dinner at seven be fine for you?" Amaury nodded. "Mr. Jones left you a mobile phone. It is lying on the table next to the sofa." Amaury looked where she pointed and saw the phone.

"Do I have to share a bath down the hall?" She shook her head.

"No, Mr. Jones insisted that you have a unit with a private bathroom with shower." They walked to the bathroom. There was a toilet and a low tub with a shower nozzle. Whenever he could bathe again, it would be a hot bubble bath. Perhaps Rawlin would join him, even though the tub was tiny.

"So that's it. The mailboxes are just beyond the desk where you found me, and you can explore the interior garden later. It's very nice in the morning and afternoon, for coffee or tea."

"Thank you, Madam."

"Sophie. Just call me Sophie. And my sister is Gillian."

"I think I'll rest now. I don't have much energy yet, from the hospital."

"Of course. Get some rest, and Gillian will be here at around 1:00 with your lunch."

Amaury thanked her again and walked her to the door, locking it behind her.

He walked over to the middle of the room and broke into a huge smile, and laughed with glee. He had a home that had nothing to do with his family!

Kicking his shoes off, he carefully lay down on the couch, pulling the throw which lay across the back, covered himself, and was soon asleep.

## Chapter 25

Rawlin's job in Montreal was textbook, wrapping up in just eight days. He packed his bags and booked a flight that would land in Lubbock, Texas, where his small ranch was located.

The whole idea of any holiday had been unappealing to Rawlin after his wife and baby's death. It meant family time, which he didn't have. Thanksgiving had come and gone in France without any celebration. Rawlin was glad.

Christmas this year was different. All Rawlin wanted was to be with Amaury, not here in Texas with his parents, sister, and her kids. And there were the ghosts that awaited him at the ranch.

Updating his parents, he placed a call to the farm in Abernathy. To his surprise, his dad picked up the phone.

"Dad? It's Rawlin. What in the world are you doing answering the house phone? You never answer the phone."

Kenneth Jones laughed like Santa at the comment. It was unusual.

"It's Wednesday, son. You know very well that your mother is at the beauty shop. She has to catch up on all of the area gossips."

"Oh my gosh, how could I forget about the beauty shop? She still goes every week, huh? That's so old-fashioned, but so is mom."

"Yep, she sure is. Are you finished with your job up there?"

"I am, and the timing is perfect if I remember the Christmas Week Calendar agenda. I land at 3:45 on Monday."

"Ah, that is perfect! Your mother will be so happy. We all will. Do you need us to pick you up, or what?"

"No. Carlos is going to be dropping my truck off on Monday morning. He's been keeping it running for me during these past years."

Carlos Vasquez has been Rawlin's ranch foreman since the day he bought the 6,000 acres the year he got married. His family, wife Alicia, twenty-four-year-old son

Miguel, and twenty-one-year-old daughter, Emisty, moved into the original house on the property so that Carlos could take better care of the horses and oversee the upkeep of the land.

"It's been about a month since I've been up there. Carlos is doing a great job with the place. Three are about to foal any day now."

"For real? That's great. I know that I can count on Carlos and his family to take care of things for me. Rawlin let the family live in the older house, rent-free, with a new truck and trailer for work and home. "I'm calling him next to tell him that I'm coming. Everything is covered up and dusty. I don't want to see it that way."

Rawling didn't want to see it at all. If he had his way, he'd sell the whole kit and kaboodle and buy another property for the horses and build a smaller house for necessity.

"I will head down to the farm on Tuesday afternoon. That way, I can take care of the place, pay respects, and be there in time to go caroling at night. Yall still do that. On Tuesday night, caroling with the church?"

"You bet we do! The church got a new bus since you were here. It's pretty nice. We ride it all over the place, then end up back at the church for hot chocolate and Christmas cookies." Rawlin remembered.

"I'll give Candi a call, too. I want her to do something at the house for me before I get there."

Rawlin let his dad go and gave Carlos a call. He kept in regular contact with the ranch due to the horse boarding business. He used to train roping horses himself, along with Carlos, his family, and the men that came and went with the seasons on the ranch.

"Hey, boss! I hear that you're coming home to Texas. Am I right, or is it a horrible rumor?" The two of them laughed.

"I'm afraid it's true. I was hoping you could bring my truck to the airport. Please leave it in short-term parking. I have my key. I'll drive it to the ranch. My flight lands at 3:45 in the afternoon."

"We'll drop it off earlier on Monday, boss. You're going to stay at the house?"

"Yes, I am." Carlos seemed as shocked as his dad was.

"But the house is closed up. Should we open it up for you? There are covers on everything. Alicia's only dusted it and kept the covers on everything these past few years."

"Yes, but hire it done unless Alicia wants to pick up some Christmas cash. I'm sure she knows someone who can clean it."

"My wife will want to do it for you and Leslie. Rawlin did. Leslie was a friend to everyone she met. They were good friends, remember?"

"Okay. How are the kids?"

Carlos told him that his son Miguel was still working with him on the ranch and his first baby boy on the way. Emisty recently graduated with an MBA from Texas Tech University in Animal Husbandry and Education

"She wants to work with animals. So she's got herself a teaching job here in

Lubbock as the Agriculture Teacher at the high school."

"That's wonderful, Carlos. I'm sure you've got everything well in hand on the ranch. Thank you for taking care of the truck. I'll see you on Monday afternoon."

Next, he called Candy. A sensitive situation needed to be taken care of, and Rawlin wanted his sister to take care of it.

## Chapter 26

Amaury carefully rolled out of bed at ten-thirty, scowling at the clock. He held his stomach, hoping it wouldn't hurt as he made his way to the bathroom. The pill must have worn off because as soon as he bent a little, his whole stomach felt a pang of pain. Damn it! The night would have been long and sleepless without the pain medicine. The pills were in the cabinet above the sink. Amaury took one and prayed it worked quickly.

After a painful session of a sponge bath and brushing teeth, Amaury pulled on a pair of joggers with a drawstring band. It would be much less painful. A fleece pull-on sweater felt so good on his skin.

Just as Amaury was about to sit on the couch, his breakfast arrived.

"Come in!" Jillian opened the door carrying a tray of assorted foods.

"Good morning, Amaury. You still look pale. You need to eat all of your food and be very careful with your stomach."

"Yes, I will. It's still quite painful, but it's only been three days since the surgery. The doctor said it would take time to build up my strength." The older woman set the try next to Amaury, handed him a fork, and stuck a napkin under his chin. "Thank you. It looks and smells wonderful." Oatmeal with honey, bananas, milk, and water would be filling but not hard on his stomach. The woman waited until he tried the oatmeal. "It's delicious." Then, she seemed satisfied and headed for the door.

Amaury turned on his Bluetooth. New Age music filled the apartment as he wondered what Rawlin was doing right now. It was seven hours ahead in Texas. It was five-thirty and almost quitting time if Rawlin's schedule was similar to his Rouen job. So why hadn't he called? Maybe he was giving Amaury time to get his passport before calling. At one-thirty today, Amaury must make his way to the train station to meet Loren and get it. He wanted to be excited about getting the passport, but until he had the document in his hands, he refused to get excited about going to Texas for Christmas.

A cow boy in Paris

The trip to the train station was a tough one. Amaury took a pain pill thirty minutes before he left so that the pain might be manageable. It was, but things were blurry, and every time Amaury misstepped, it jarred his body, and the pain shot through him.

Amaury found a spot on a bench where Loren would see him as soon as he stepped off the train. As he waited, he dared to dream of what going to Texas would be. Rawlin would be introducing him to his family.

Adrenaline helped the pain dull a bit. It would be short-lived.

Amaury stood as the one-thirty train pulled into the station. As each person got off the train and it wasn't Loren, nervousness replaced hope. Amaury was in tears when the last person on the stop got off. He didn't come. Now what? Maybe he missed the train. Amaury waited for the following two trains to arrive before giving up and returning to the apartment. He cried all the way.

Amaury wanted to call Rawlin and tell him what was happening, but he didn't know himself. Why hadn't Loren come with his passport? There could be two reasons. Amalie had problems with the baby, or his father wouldn't let Loren take the passport.

Deciding to sleep so he wouldn't have to think, the knock on his door at seven o'clock woke him. It was his dinner arriving. He barely spoke two words to the older woman, and Amaury played with his mashed potatoes and chopped steak more than he ate.

Sponge bath completed and dressed in his pajamas, Amaury climbed into bed carefully and closed his eyes. The mobile ringing jolted him awake from a soft slumber. It was Loren

## Chapter 27

After speaking to his dad and Carlos, Rawlin called his sister a couple of hours later. She seemed to be in a gloomy mood. Rawlin needed her help but became more concerned and asked what was happening with her and the kids.

"Josie hates me. She called me fatso. Said she's having sex with that man who's older than you tonight. She came over here to get some of the things that she left behind the night she left home."

"I'm sorry, Candy. Where was Linus during all of this? I hope he wasn't there."

"Thankfully, he was over at that sissy friend of his house. I can't believe I just said that. I don't want him over there, turning gay." Rawlin had to say it.

"Candy, you don't turn someone gay. They just are. And don't be that way."

"What way? I don't want him being beaten up or mistreated, Rawlin. Who'd wish that upon their kid?" Rawlin's throat got dry. He agreed with her.

"I'll be there tomorrow night. Why don't you bring them over, and I'll talk to them a little bit." Candy was relieved. She must think he was this great role model or something. If only she knew. Well, she would soon if he brought Amaruy over to Texas.

Rawlin needed to phone Amaury. Surely by now, he had his passport, knew if he could get it, or was required to apply for a new one. For now, he had a little problem of his own.

"Candy, I need a favor. Have your kids help you with it if you want. Carlos and Alicia are going to the house to uncover and dust the place. I need something more from you." Rawlin wondered if she was guessing what he was going to ask. "I haven't been in that house since after the funeral. It's got my wife all over it. I just can't go in there with it like that."

"I understand completely. Tell me what you need us to do, and we'll take care of it."

Rawlin asked her to remodel the place. Remove all of the feminine touches that Leslie had put into place. Curtains, bed sets, rugs, decorated towels, knickknacks, and photos.

"Rawlin, what about the Nursery? It's just as you both left it." Rawlin was already shaking his head to himself.

"No. Leave that room for me to do. It's the right thing to do. Leslie might be haunting that room." He faked a little laugh at his comment. "Baby Mattie needs her dad to take care of her things."

"I agree. It's time. I promise we will do a great job decorating your home, brother."

"You mean my house. That is not my home, Candy. I guess you could say that I'm homeless just as much as my friend in Paris was, just in a different way."

"Is this the friend you are bringing to Texas?"

"I hope so. I am waiting to see if their passport is up valid."

"I'd love to meet anyone who's a friend of my brother. I'm glad you've met someone new, Rawlin. No one should be alone. We need one another."

J. M Palmer

"I think you might be right."

## Chapter 28

Loren apologized for not being at the train station. Amaury waited to hear which one of the two reasons he'd been right, for Loren's not showing up.

"I found your passport in the house safe. I took it out and was about to close the safe when your father walked in." Amaury scowled at the idea that this man was his father.

"Your father-in-law wouldn't let you take my passport with you, would he?"

"No. I'm sorry, Amaury. Pierre said if you want it, you have to come and get it yourself. I don't know what he did with it, either. But, again, I'm very sorry."

"It's not your fault, Loren. Thank you for trying."

"What are you going to do now?" Amaury told Loren that he couldn't go to the vineyards. He would apply for a new passport. He'd have to wait until a new one came in to go to the states if he went at all.

"Did you tell Amalie about this? I hope not since she's delicate with the pregnancy." Loren said that he hadn't, and neither had their father.

"Thank you for that. No reason to worry her. "I want you to call me whenever Amalie has the baby. I want to know that everything is okay. My number is on your caller-id. I didn't block it on purpose. Don't give it to anyone else, especially your in-laws. Clear your phone calls. I don't want him to know that I called you at all." Loren agreed to all of it. They said their goodbyes, and Amaury laid down to rest again.

All that Amaury could do now was wait for Rawlin to call. Surely he would do just that tomorrow. He worried about Rawlin changing his mind about being with him after being home for a while. And he has good reason.

## Chapter 29

Rawlin landed at Lubbock International Airport on time. It was snowing lightly. Rawlin was happy to reunite with his Ford King Ranch Edition, four-wheel-drive. It could drive in any weather.

The ranch was just over thirty minutes away from the airport. Rawlin felt like an alien as he went the main highway and turned onto the Farm to Market road that led to the ranch.

Country music played softly in the cab, interrupted by an occasional weather report on local radio. It was surreal. Rawlin felt a knot in his stomach the whole way from the airport until he laid eyes on the red brock, a colonial house that used to be his home.

Carlos had done an excellent job keeping the place up. Winter landscaping in the front plots, neatly trimmed, have snow collecting on each scrub on the side of the porch.

Rawlin parked the truck under the cover to the side of the house and killed the engine. The sight of the house took him back in time. He could picture Leslie, her large belly, and himself hurrying inside to get out of the snow. It seemed a million years ago.

Taking a deep breath, Rawlin got out of the truck, heading for the front door. He had to get this return to his house over.

The key opened quickly, and warmth from the fireplace rushed at Rawlin as he came inside. Carlos or Candy must have lit it for him.

The living room looked different. Candy and the kids had done an excellent job making the place look different. The florals and bright furniture Leslie had picked for their new home were Gone. In its place were dark greens, maroons, and browns. It looked like a man's house.

Over the mantle, Rawlin was happy to see the oil portrait of he and Leslie had been removed. Cany had wrapped it, as asked so that Rawlin could gift it to Leslie's parents. He didn't want it. Too many sad memories. Besides, he had the photo on which the oil portrait was based, in a smaller size.

A painting of a cowboy on his horse had replaced it.

In the kitchen, gone were the cat curtains and knickknacks chosen by Leslie. Instead, a lovely pale blue theme graced the kitchen now. It fit perfectly in a cowboy's house.

Down the hall, Rawlin saw that the guestroom bedding was new, and the bathroom was gold and green instead of sea turtles.

Besides the nursery, the master bedroom would be the worst reminder of what had been. Rawlin walked past the nursery with a closed-door into his bedroom.

A vibrant purple southwest quilt covered the bed. Rawlin owed his sister a massive thanks. He'd been afraid he couldn't even sleep in this room if it was the same as he left it. At least he could, now.

The bathroom was turquoise and purple, with fresh towels, soap, and toothpaste for Rawlin. He nodded his head.

Bringing his luggage into the bedroom, Rawlin began to relax a little bit.

He needed to hang his clothes and see what needed to be pressed if it was too wrinkled.

His heart leaped as he opened the door. Nor he or Candy had thought about the closet. It was filled with Leslie and the baby's clothes. Rawlin fingered the ruffles on one of his wife's blouses and pulled out a blue satin baby dress. Looking at it brought on sudden tears of grief. Rawlin was so overcome he had to sit on the bed. Tulip Lee Jones died in the crash at seven months, twenty-one days old. They were going to call her Tullie. The flower was both his and Leslie's favorite. The funeral was filled with tulips from family and friends who knew the planned name and its significance.

Rawlin texted Candy and his mother to let them know that he had arrived and planned to come over the next day, and he'd see them then. Josie and Linus could come over at tenish so that he could talk to them about everything if they wanted to.

Finished unpacking, Rawlin wanted to talk to Carlos and see the horses. So he put his coat and workboots on and rode the Kawasaki Mule in the garage, down to the old house. Carlos came out the front door as

Rawlin pulled to a stop. The snow was still falling, but it was still light.

"Rawlin! Old friend." The two men hugged. Carlos had been working in one form or another on the Jones' properties since Rawlin was thirteen years old.

"Carlos, the house looks great! You've taken good care of it. Where's Alicia?"

"She's at Emisty's apartment in town. I told her not to drive home tonight. You'll see them tomorrow. Come on. I know you want to see the horses. We've got two about to foal." Rawlin told him that's what his dad had said. They took the Mule out to the stables. "We're boarding 35 horses right now. It's been pretty busy around here. Four of those foaled last month alone!" Rawlin was pleased. The ranch had always done well financially, and Rawlin invested well. He wasn't rich, but he could retire tomorrow and live a good life for the rest of his years if he chose to.

"How's Blaze? He's going on nine now. You still riding him for me?" The blaze was Rawlin's favorite paint.

"He's great! Still got an attitude just like his owner in his younger days."

Rawlin laughed.

"I've mellowed, Carlos." Then, speaking to himself, he said, "I wish you were here to ride Blaze." He laughed.

"What was that, Rawlin?" He's a little embarrassed.

"A friend of mine in Paris. He wants to see and ride my horses. He's never ridden." Carlos nodded, assuming he meant a woman. Everyone would.

After looking over the horses, Rawlin took Blaze on a quick ride. The horse snuggled up to Rawlin and bobbed his head up and down.

"Amaury would love you, boy! He is an amazing young man who you'll fall in love with, too." Rawlin headed the horse to the stalls, handing him over to Carlos, and headed back into the house. It was time to call Amaury to find out about the passport.

## Chapter 30

Amaury was in a deep sleep whenever the phone began to ring. It had to be Rawlin. Who else would be calling the number at two-forty-five?

"Rawlin? He could hardly contain his emotions.

"Hi, baby. It's me. I'm sorry it took me so long to call, but I wanted to give you time to get that drain out before I called. So is it out, and how are you feeling?"

"I feel well, but my diet is still mild for a while. I still get my meals made by the ladies here. It's good food even though it's bland." Rawlin was glad to hear it. He just wanted Amaury to be off the streets and safe. "I miss you so much, cowboy. Nothing is the same without you." Rawlin didn't say anything, so he continued. "I have bad news regarding my passport."

"What's wrong?" Rawlin had severe doubts about having Amaury come over for the holidays. Candy's comments about Linus' friend didn't help.

Amaury told Rawlin what happened when Loren tried to get his passport, and Amaury was too scared of his father to ask for it.

"We'll have to apply for a new one, baby. Besides, the timing is all wrong. My sister is in the middle of a divorce and needs me to help with her teenagers, and my parents are getting older, and there are a dozen things that need repairs at the farm." Amaury was getting the picture. The passport was the perfect excuse not to fly him to Texas. He had to see if this was true.

"Rawlin, go get my passport. If you aren't afraid to come out to your family and introduce me as your boyfriend, the passport is the only way I can come over."

"It's not that simple, Amaury. I'm not afraid." Amaury was ready to hang up.

"At least I'm brave enough to admit that I'm scared to go get my passport. Pierre won't give it to me if I go, even though he said that I have to come."

"Amaury, give me a break. I got you an apartment. I'm paying your bills. You're off the streets and safe. If that's not showing you how much I care." Amaury cut him off.

"Stop, Rawlin. I don't need you. I was fine before you, and I'll be fine after you. Have a Merry Christmas. Goodbye." Amaury hung up the phone and sobbed.

Rawlin called him back dozens of times, leaving voicemails until Amaury's mailbox was full.

It would be a lonely Christmas. Something told Rawlin they could never return to the way things were now. Perhaps he'd find Amaury whenever he returned to Europe and be forgiven.

## Chapter 31

Amaury cried back to sleep, heartbroken. And when he woke at nine o'clock that morning, he opened the messenger bag and began to pack. As much as he loved Rawlin, this was not the happily ever after he dreamed. He supposed he'd never have it, just like his friends told him.

No more tears to cry. Amaury turned the mobile phone off and checked all the drawers to ensure he didn't leave anything behind. That's when he found the burner phone with the pictures, most of which he didn't even know existed. Amaury looked through the photos with longing. Why Rawlin? Why had he given Amaury hope at a love-filled life together? He threw the phone against the wall, which smashed into several pieces. Amaury screamed out in frustration. It sent the front desk attendant, Bonni, to his room.

"I'm very sorry. I was upset, and I screamed out in anger. I am moving out. I have packed. Everything that I leave belongs to Mr. Jones."

"But your lease is paid for six months, Amaury. Are you sure that you want to move out?" Yes, he was sure.

"Do you have an envelope that I can mail two phones to Mr. Jones?" She said that she did, down at the desk. "Thank you. I'll be leaving as soon as I address the envelope."

Amaury used the Lubbock address on the lease agreement and put the two phones inside. He thought about writing a note to Rawlin, but nothing else to say.

"Please do me one favor. Do not inform Mr. Jones of my departure. Let him get the phones in the mail, and he will understand." They agreed, and Amaury walked out of the apartment building.

The first thing he had to do was rent a locker for his stuff since he had no home once again. He hated the idea of using any of the money Rawlin had given him, but he had none. Not working while he was recovering had taken its toll.

Relieved of his stuff and the messenger bag, Amaury strolled the streets wondering what he would do until night came and the men looking were out cruising. He'd sketch! Yes. That's just what would take Rawlin off of his mind and out of his heart.

Retrieving his pad and sketching pencils, Amaury headed for the banks of the Seine, where he knew the tourists would be looking to a sitting during their Christmas holiday.

## Chapter 32

Rawlin was left stunned and still holding the phone when Amaury told him goodbye. What had just happened? Their arrangement was acceptable before. Why not now? It was just another tantrum of Amaury's. He was easy to anger but easier to forgive. Or was he? Rawlin could only wait and see.

Later that morning, Josie and Linus came by to visit with Rawlin. It was hard to believe that little Josie was the same age as Rawlin. She seemed so much younger. Linus was seventeen and cute as a boy can be. Josie looked like her mother when she was in her twenties. Linus looked like neither of his parents, but he seemed more mature than Josie. Neice and nephew came into the house and sat on the couch. It had been four years since they'd seen their uncle.

"I am so happy to see both of you! I'm sorry that I've been away so many years. I couldn't make myself come back here after what happened, but I missed out on so much of your lives."

"We totally understand, Uncle Rawly." Rawlin laughed at the sound of Linus' nickname for him. Unable to pronounce Rawlin as a youngster, this is what he'd become. "I can't imagine how sad you must have been to lose your family," Linus told him. Josie quickly changed the subject.

"How do you like the house? We all helped with redecorating. It was fun, and I'm glad we could help."

"It's perfect, Josie. I appreciate the effort you all went to. Is the painting of Leslie and me wrapped and in the garage?" Rawlin hadn't looked.

"Yes, it is. Mom said that it was for Leslie's parents. Is that right?" Rawlin nodded. "It makes me too sad to see it, and I figured they'd like to have it." Josie nodded.

"Your dad moved out. How's that been for you two? Josie practically rolled her eyes at him. It was a pretty lame thing to say. "I just mean that I don't want you to have to hear or see any of that. If they argued all the time and were unhappy, it's for the best." It makes it harder not to take sides."

"Mom let herself go and stopped trying to be a good wife, Rawlin. Dad didn't want to stay anymore." Rawlin told him that it wasn't always that simple.

"Dad got a girlfriend that's not much older than you, Josie. Mom didn't deserve that. Even if she did gain a bunch of weight, maybe she did because she's unhappy. We don't know. She never told us anything. Rawlin, Dad just up and moved out without a word. He left mom to explain. She didn't."

"Your mom told me that she's going to have a long talk with each one of you soon. I want to know what you've been up to and if I can help. I'm a great listener."

Josie told Rawlin about Barry, the twenty-six-year-old man she's dating, and how she thought about dropping out of college. Rawlin told her how important an education was and the freedom it gave you. She listened for a while before asking if she could ride Rose, her favorite horse.

Alone, Linus quickly opened up to Rawlin. There was an instant bond between the two of them.

"You've got to help me with mom. She's going crazy over this divorce and won't stay out of my personal life. She hates my friend Kerry, and I don't get why."

"Your mom told me that she's worried about your relationship with Kerry. He's kind of feminine, and she thinks he might be gay. Is he? It's not a problem for me if he is. She's concerned about how close the two of you are getting since you're so young." Linus laughed.

"That's not why she's worried, and yes, he is gay, but so am I, Uncle Rawly. I knew you'd be cool about it, so I wanted to talk to you about it. So is Josie. It's my mom and dad who are homophobes. What do I do?" Rawlin put a hand on his nephew's shoulder and squeezed it.

"I envy you in so many ways, Linus. You aren't afraid of who you are, and you know what you want. Is Kerry your boyfriend?" Linus nodded. "I thought so. You don't need to pretend you're someone you aren't."

"I won't do that. How can anyone live like that? It would drive me insane!"

"Linus, your generation is much more open-minded than mine was. I did what I thought was expected of me. I was supposed to marry a woman, have kids, and live in a brick house with a two-car garage. Well, I did that, but it wasn't who I was. Or who I am." Linus looked at him eye to eye for a moment.

"Oh my gosh! You're gay like me, aren't you? Does mom know?" Rawlin shook his head.

"Yes, I am gay, and no, your mom doesn't have a clue. I married Leslie, and I loved her, but I was never in love with her. I shouldn't have married her. It wasn't fair to her, and I don't know if she figured it out or not. I hope not. It was wrong to lie to her, but I tried so hard to be straight. The church and my family told me it was wrong to be gay, but it's not. It's who I am." Rawlin hugged Linus. "I can talk to your mom if you want me to."

"Would you? That would be awesome! I love Kerry. We're both going to go to Rice University instead of Tech. Houston is much friendlier to gay people, and it will give me a bit of privacy from mom."

"I think that's a great idea. However, you need a bit of distance to become yourself in college."

"We could come out together," Linus suggested, but Rawlin didn't think it was a good idea.

"I appreciate your trust and confidence in me, but I'm a big failure in this area, kiddo. I left the love of my life back in Paris because I'm afraid of what my family will think when I show up with a boyfriend and explain that I'm gay and in love with a man."

"They might surprise you. Mom is hard, but Nana and Papa are all about unconditional love, ya know? So I think they'll be easier."

"I hope you're right, but I remember all of the comments and jokes Papa made throughout the years, so I don't know."

"Only one way to find out." The kid was right. "I'm going to come out on Christmas Eve. Think about it and tell them at the same time. If they're against it, then we can deal with it together." Another hug from

Rawlin and Linus was feeling on top of the world.

"I'm inviting Kerry to come along for family Christmas week. I won't do the activities without him."

"Bring him. You should! I'm proud of you, Linus. You're quite the young man."

"Thanks, Uncle Rawlin." It was the first time Linus had used his real name.

The kids were gone. Rawlin had Carlos get them a pizza while he was in town. Rawlin ate and tried to call Amaury again, which went straight to a recording saying the caller was unavailable. He's turned the phone off. That was not good news.

In bed in his ranch house, Rawlin felt the empty side of the bed and told Amaury goodnight out loud. Then, after looking at the photos of the two of them together, he turned out the lights and went to sleep.

## Chapter 33

While Amaruy was living on the streets again, working, and taking care of himself, Rawlin was busy with family Christmas week. So on Tuesday night, Rawlin put on a red shirt for caroling, got in his truck, and headed for Abernathy and the family farm twenty miles away. It was cold in the panhandle that night, but the snow was holding off for now, so the roads weren't too bad.

As the Ford parked in front of the farmhouse, Sammie Jones ran out to greet her son with a big hug and tears.

"Rawlin, my baby!" She was crushing him with a hug when his dad, Kenneth, walked up, followed by Candy and the kids.

"Mama, your gonna break him! Look how skinny that boy is." Kenneth offered a hand, which Rawlin took but also hugged his dad, no matter how sissy it was. Rawlin didn't care.

"Dad! Mama! You both look great!" They did, for their age, in their sixties. Working on a farm and ranch aged a body. Candy walked forward. Rawlin barely recognized his sister with the added weight. He could tell that she was embarrassed by her looks. Rawlin hugged her tightly. "It's so good to be home, sis." Candy was crying and didn't let go of Rawlin.

"Hi, Uncle Rawlin," Linus said, and then Josie. The blonde-haired, blue-eyed boy with long lashes had to be Kerry. "This is Kerry, the guy I told you about." Rawlin extended his hand, which Kerry softly shook.

"It's great to meet you, Kerry. I'm glad you decided to come." Rawlin gave Candy a look. She returned a confused one. He wouldn't tell Linus' news. Let the boy do it himself. Rawlin wanted the boyfriend to feel welcome to church caroling.

"Hi, Rawlin. I've heard all about you from Linus." Linus winked at Rawlin.

"Uh, oh. That can't be good!" They all laughed as snow began to fall.

"We've got to get over to the church. The buses will be loaded soon! Candy, get the cocoa and cookies. Josie, help her, will you?" Josie and Candy headed inside to get the treats.

The family gathered with the congregation at the Baptist Church and shared prayer, holding hands. Rawlin met old friends and new people, who divided and boarded two charter buses with heaters. They would drive the neighborhood, get out, sing carols, and do it over again and again until they reached the church again. Then, they'd have cocoa, eat cookies, visit a while and go their separate ways.

It might have been a fun night if Amaury had been there with him. Instead, he was all that Rawlin could think about. *I want to be with Amaury right now and nowhere else.*

In Paris, Amaury made good money from sketches and men, and he tried hard to enjoy Christmas lights, music, and celebrations. But, without Rawlin by his side, it meant nothing. Nothing was the same anymore. Living on the streets and doing

## A cow boy in Paris

what he wanted when he wanted to was suddenly the loneliest life there was.

Amaury often wondered what Rawlin was doing and cursed himself for doing so. Why had he ever set his sights on the cowboy in the first place?

## Chapter 34

Rawlin was acting his way through the week. After a night of caroling, the family attended a production of The Nutcracker at The Lubbock Performing Arts Center on Wednesday night, a drive-in movie of "It's a Wonderful life', and a party Thursday night was the City of Abernathy's Christmas Festival Celebration. On Friday, these days leading up to Christmas Eve left Rawlin sitting at the family farm in Abernathy. He would be spending the night. It was a family tradition for them all to wake up together in the house on Christmas Day morning.

The ladies were busy making the lunch, and Linus pulled up with Kerry.

Rawlin watched Candy walk to the door, unhappy that this boy was at the family home. He stopped his sister from going out to tell her son to take Kerry home.

"Candy, don't. Stay in the house and let your son bring Kerry to lunch with the family. Who's it going to hurt if Linus has a guest?" Candy backed off, but she wasn't happy.

"Having that boy here can hurt my son, Rawlin. I'll let it go because it's Christmas, but that's the only reason." Linus and Kerry walked into the house.

"Merry Christmas, everyone!" Linus tried to be nonchalant. Rawlin helped.

"Merry Christmas, Linus, and Kerry!" Linus hugs his uncle and whispers. "It's on," meaning that he's going to come out as planned.

"It's all good," Rawlin whispered back. It would be a big moment whenever Linus told the family he was gay and Kerry was his boyfriend.

As the group sat around doing their tasks, from cooking, baking, making Christmas Ornaments, etc., Rawlin felt more and more empty without Amaury.

Slipping into the bedroom, he tried once again to phone Amaury. No. The phone was still turned off. After he ended the call, a text alert came in that a package had been delivered to his ranch house. Rawlin found Linus and Kerry.

"Hey, will you guys go over to my house to get a package that just got delivered? I'm pretty sure it's a gift for your Nana. Open it up and make sure it's a necklace, okay?"

"Sure. We can do that. And when we get back, I think I'm going to make my announcement. I'll need your support if things get weird."

"You've got it. Hurry over and back. I need to wrap and slip it under the tree before we go to bed tonight."

The boys told their mom why they were leaving. While they were gone, Rawlin had a little talk with his sister about being open-minded. It seemed to have her thinking. This was good.

Amaury put on his best clothes for Christmas, hoping to pick up a client who might have a little more money and have a nice hotel room. He ended up doing better than that. The Englishman he found needed an escort to Don Quixote: Paris Opera Ballet at the Opera Bastille, a favorite of Amaury's. When the man took him to a tailor's shop to get a suit of clothes, Amaury almost cried. It reminded him of his day with Rawlin and when they'd gone clothes shopping.

Amaury ended with a pair of grey trousers, a black vest, and a paisley gray and white button shirt. He also got socks and black dress shoes.

"He will need a matching jacket," the client told the tailor, "and a black beret."

It was so cliché' but Amaury loved berets. He knew he wore them well.

His hair in a knot, Amaury looked very proper and ready for the play. The client, Jeremy, was delighted, telling him that he could keep the clothes after conducting business at the hotel.

Rawlin talked with his dad about jobs overseas and future work, and they almost argued about Rawlin continuing to work in Europe. But, instead, Rawlin went through the motions, and his mother noticed and had a seat next to him.

"Son, your mind is a million miles away from here. Or is it just thousands?" Rawlin smiled at her, almost tearing up. All he could manage was a nod. "Why didn't you bring your friend from Paris with you? I'm sure you're missing them."

"You have no idea, mom. It was a problem with their passport. And it just didn't seem to be the right time for an introduction." The doorbell interrupted their conversation.

As if things couldn't get any more stressful, they did. The guests at the door were Leslie's parents. Candy had invited them so that Rawlin could give them the painting of him and Leslie. Rawlin hadn't seen them since the gathering at his house after the funeral. So he stood when they came over to say their hello's.

Donald and Sarah Matten looked much older than their mid-sixties years. The death of their daughter and granddaughter had been very hard on them. Rawlin's leaving made it even worse, according to his mother. Rawlin wanted to turn and run out the door right now.

"Hello, Don. Sarah. It's been a long time. I'm sorry that I haven't been in touch with you at all since Leslie's been gone. Unfortunately, I have my way of dealing with it all."

"We understand, Rawlin. For a long time, we didn't deal with it at all. We went to a Grief Counselor, which helped us a lot. You should try it." Rawlin winced. His family had tried to get him to a counselor. But, no, it wasn't something Rawlin was going to try.

"Maybe I will, Sarah." Candy walked over to them, carrying the painting. Rawlin took it. "I have something for you. I think it belongs with your family, now." Don carefully remove the wrapping paper, and the two are brought to tears. They each hugged Rawlin, who felt so bad that no tears would fall. The gifting of this painting made him feel as if this chapter of his life was finally closed.

Sammie and Kenneth could see that Rawlin needed rescuing, so they busied their lunch guests with the family preparations. Rawlin was grateful, heading outside while waiting for Linus and Kerry to return.

Not long after, Rawlin saw the blue Chevy Colorado truck pulling into the driveway. The boys brought the opened box to him.

"It's not the necklace, Rawlin. It's from Amaury in Paris. There are two phones. One is smashed." Rawlin's heart raced as he took the box. Amaury had held this box.

"Did the phone get broken in the mail?" Kerry asked Rawlin. He shook his head.

"No. Amaury broke it on purpose. He's upset with me."

"He's your boyfriend, isn't he?" Rawlin nodded again.

"Yes, Linus. Rawlin pulled out his phone, pulling up a photo of Amaury. "This is him. Isn't he beautiful? He is my boyfriend." Linus whistled. "Come on. Let's go. It's time to make announcements."

"Alright!" Linus yelled, and the three men headed for the house.

Inside, Rawlin got everyone's attention for Linus.

## A cow boy in Paris

"I need everyone's attention, please. Linus has something he wants to say, and so do I." Linus stepped up, taking Kerry by the hand. He yelled out his sexuality.

"Mom, everybody, I'm gay, and this is my boyfriend, Kerry. He is going to be around for a while. Please treat him like a member of the family."

When Candy started to say something negative, Rawlin took his turn.

"Don't any of you treat this boy any differently than you did before he made this announcement unless it's positive?" He looked from his dad to his mom and Candy and the kids. "I'm leaving. I shouldn't be here without Amaury. He's in Paris, but he was supposed to be here with me for Christmas. Yes, it's a guy. I've known I'm gay since I was in college." Rawlin gave a sympathetic look to the Matten's. "I'm flying to Paris to get the young man that I'm in love with and bring him back here to meet my family." Rawlin headed for the door, leaving shocked looks around the room. "Linus, fill people in. I'll send you a few photos to show everyone. I'll see all of you whenever I return."

J. M Palmer

Jumping into his Ford, Rawlin sped out of the driveway and toward his house. First, he had to grab his passport, pack a carry-on, book a flight, and head for the airport.

## Chapter 35

Amaury was in a better mood after attending the play and having a client who didn't treat him like street trash. So, with money in his pocket and wearing his fancy clothes, Amaury decided to treat himself to a nice brunch. He'd slept in an unlocked storage room at the Gare de Lyon train station.

He washed up in the men's room and found a table to eat some poached eggs, toast, and fruit. Amaury still had to take it easy on his stomach,

Since it was Christmas Eve morning, half as many people were out and about. So Amaury decided not to work unless he found an exceptional client. Instead, he would walk the streets and ride the rails through Paris, enjoying the Christmas lights and decorations. The sad moments were whenever he saw a couple holding hands.

It was fifty degrees on this beautiful holiday as Amaury walked the streets looking at the shop windows and the families enjoying the holiday. He had no idea that Rawlin returned at six-thirty that morning and had been frantically looking for him.

Rawlin started in the train station where he'd first met Amaury and proceeded to go to every place he'd ever seen Amaury or gone to with him. It was all to no avail. There was no sign of his beautiful young man. Rawlin only stopped to get a bite to eat at one of the few cafes open on Christmas Eve. Then the search continued.

Coming full circle, Rawlin ended up back at the railway station, where he found bench viewing arrivals. It was almost one o'clock, and he had been looking since the ride into the city on the train from Charles De Gaul. His feet ached, and he felt a determination he'd never felt before. He would find Amaury even if it took him weeks to do so.


Amaury had avoided any areas where he'd gone with Rawlin, for he feared the emotional response would overwhelm him. But today, on Christmas Eve, Amaury wanted to feel close to the cowboy. He'd taken the train to the station where Rawlin finally had the nerve to ask Amaury to go for a coffee with him and ran away, scared.

It was almost two o'clock now, and Rawlin's trip and jet lag were wearing on him now. As he watched the trains come and go without a sign of Amaury, his eyes grew heavy. Finally, when the 2:15 train pulled into the station, Rawlin decided to stand and walk to stay awake. It might be time for an espresso.

The train was packed, and Amaury stood holding the bar, ready to disembark with the first wave of passengers.

Rawlin paced back and forth as the train pulled into the station, saying a prayer to himself that Amaury was on the train. Was it wrong to ask God?

Rawlin was beginning to get disappointed after about thirty people got off, and then he saw a black beret and familiar brown eyes. Did he see things, or was Amaury there walking among the crowd?

Amaury was trying to make his way through the people. He had no idea what he was going to do for Christmas. The mobile phone

Rawlin had given him would come in handy. He wanted to know if the baby had been born.

Looking up, Amaury saw a cowboy hat amongst the people. Exhaustion from a busy day of walking around must have been getting to him. But the more he studied the distant figure, he was sure. The urgency in the man's walk made Amaury hurry.

Rawlin could see Amaury's face now, and his heart ached with love. Please don't turn me away, he thought.

Rawlin needn't have worried, for as soon as he's sure not hallucinating, Amaury begins to run toward his lover.

As the two met, Amaury jumped into Rawlin's waiting arms and spun around as the two shared a passionate kiss. Rawlin was no longer worried about what people would think or say. He kissed Amaury again.

"I'm so sorry, baby. I missed you so much I couldn't stand it!"

"Me, too! I do forgive you because I understand your actions, my love."

They moved over to a bench to sit and talk. "You wear your cowboy hat for me?"

"Yes. I hope you see me and do not run away. I am in love with you, Amaury. For the first time, I am in love, and I'm never gonna let you go." They hugged.

"Do I have your promise? I am in love with you, too! I give you all of my freedom, and I will wake up with you every morning that the Gods allow!"

"Amaury, let's go get your passport. You are coming to Texas with me.

## Chapter 36

The train ride out to Reims would take the boys 46 minutes, according to the schedule. They didn't talk much on the way. Amaury's head rested on Rawlin's shoulder. The older man had an arm protectively around the younger man's shoulder.

Rawlin had no plan of how things would go whenever they arrived at Rousseau Vinyards. But they weren't leaving without the passport.

The closer the train got to Reims, the more nervous Amaury became. Rawlin could feel him trembling with fear.

"Amaury, this man can't hurt you while you're with me. I won't let him. I'll stand between the two of you if I have to." He kissed Amaury's forehead.

After departing the train, Rawlin summoned an Uber driver to take them to the vineyard. They hoped Loren would drive them back to the train station.

The driveway to the winery was long and winding. Amaury had some positive memories of his early life at this place. Unfortunately, things went to hell whenever Arnaud got sick when he was sixteen and Amaury was fourteen. And to top it all off, Pierre caught Amaury making out with a boy in his bedroom. He wasn't the first, just the boy Amaury was seen with. The ultimatum was given at that time. Leave boys or leave home. Amaury left.

The house was a mansion, surprising Rawlin. It looked like a cathedral with gothic looks and iron gates. Amaury looked at his open mouth and remembered how intimidating the house could be.

"Rawlin, it is okay. We do very well by the champagne, okay? This

vineyard is the fifth generation." Rawlin nodded and swallowed hard. The passport was somewhere in that fortress. How was he supposed to get in there and get the paper out?"

The Uber deposited the two men at the smaller, similarly styled house at the bottom of the hill. A new Audi sedan sat in front of the house, and a Pomeranian dog barked viciously at Rawlin and Amaury. The Uber drive departed, and the noise caused someone from inside the place to come out.

"Amaury?" It was Loren, his brother-in-law. "Is that you?" The man turned back to the house, calling his wife, "Amalie! Your brother is here! Come quickly!" A pregnant young woman appeared at the door.

"Oh my gosh! Amaury!" The young lady and her husband hurried to Amaury, enveloping him in hugs and kisses. Rawlin stepped aside to let them reunite.

His attention back on Rawlin, Amaury proudly introduced the Texan.

"This is my boyfriend, Rawlin. He's from Texas, and he's taking me there to visit with him." Amaury hooked arms with Rawlin. Rawlin shook Loren's hand and gently hugged Amalie.

"It's very nice to meet you both. Amaury is lucky to have you in his corner.

Thank you for that." Amalie gave Rawlin a kiss, kiss on his cheeks.

"He is my brother. I love my little brother, and I am delighted to meet the man in his life. It would help if you took good care of this boy. He's a wonderful person."

"You have my promise that I'll take good care of him, Amalie." He looked at her belly. "When is the baby coming?" She smiled, rubbing her round figure.

"I have two months to go. He is already a big boy! I'm ready for Arnaud Amaury to enter the world." Rawlin praised Amaury's sister for the name choice.

They were talking, catching up whenever a grumpy voice came from inside the house, chilling Rawlin to the bone. But Amaury squealed with glee.

"Papi!" He ran to the older man, who gave him a bear hug. Amaury was soon in tears, as was the man. Amalie explained that Papi is their Grandfather on the paternal side. Amaury pulled his Papi to Rawlin, introducing him. "This man is my Papi. I haven't seen him since I was sixteen." Rawlin shook the man's hand.

"It's great to meet you, sir. You sure have an amazing grandson." The older man smiled quizzically at Rawlin.

"You are much older than my Grandson. How old are you, Mr. Jones?"

"I'm twenty-eight years old, and I love Amaury. You may rest assured that I am not taking advantage of him and will protect him with my life, sir." Papi Henri looked him over head to toe and nodded.

"I believe that you will, Rawl, was it?" Amaury laughed, correcting him.

"I never thought I'd see you at the vineyard again, brother, and especially with a boyfriend. Why have you come?"

"Your father would not let Loren bring Amaury's passport to Paris for him. I'd planned to take him to Lubbock to meet my family and spend Christmas with them."

Loren explained what had happened when he'd tried to take the passport from the safe in the main house.

"You said nothing of this to me, Loren. Why not?" Amalie didn't look happy.

"I didn't want to emotionally upset you, darling. You are so delicate now and with your history of pregnancies. I didn't want to take a chance." She understood but was very angry with her controlling father.

"Papa doesn't want you here if you care for boys, but he holds your passport hostage? He is a mean-hearted man to you!"

"We want the passport, and we'll leave. I don't want any trouble, but your father told Loren that Amaury had to come to get the passport if he wanted it, so here he is."

A golf cart came speeding along, parking next to the Audi as they talked. Rawlin looked to Amaury to confirm his suspicions. The man was none other than Pierre.

Amaury walked to Rawlin, standing next to him as Pierre got out of the cart.

"Lots of commotion for a couple of visitors down here, isn't it?" He looked at Amaury and Rawlin.

"The prodigal returns. Hmph. And who is this that you bring with you?"

Rawlin hated the man who made his love so miserable and felt unworthy.

"I'm Rawlin Jones. Amaury is my boyfriend. We are here to get his passport, and then we will leave your vineyard and never come back." The look of arrogance on Pierre Rousseau's face disgusted Rawlin.

"The passport is mine. I paid for it, and it belongs to a son I no longer have."

Amaury stepped up to Pierre after gaining a bit of confidence through Rawlin.

"You told Loren if I wanted my passport, I had to come to get it myself. I did. Please give it to me. I'll pay you if I need to for the fees."

Pierre slapped Amaury on the face so hard it knocked him to the ground without warning. Rawlin was on him in an instant pinning Piere's arm behind him.

"Don't you ever touch him again! I won't tolerate it. Give him the damned passport so we can get out of this damned place." Whenever Piere refused, Rawlin tightened his grip. "I could snap your arm easily, jackass."

"I will call Security to bring the Police for assault." Rawlin laughed.

"Go right ahead. I can see the headlines. 'Pierre Rousseau assaulted by gay son's Texas Boyfriend.' You've tried to hide that you have a gay son and had one who committed suicide from not getting help for being bipolar. I'll make sure I mention that fact to everyone who interviews me." He let go of Rousseau by pushing him forward. He fell to his knees.

Amaury was crying, Pierre was hollering, and all hell was breaking loose when Papa Henri cleared his throat to get their attention.

"All of you, stop this right now! We are adults here. Let's act like it." He looked at his son. "Pierre, you disappoint me many times in your life, but mostly over these boys, Arnaud and Amaury. They did not need to be perfect to be a Rousseau. You weren't."

"Papa, no. Do not continue with this talk. Amaury and his male friend need to leave," Henri said.

"Piere has something to prove. He had many speech problems as a child to overcome." Suddenly a woman appeared from the shadows. It was Mallory, Amalie, and Amaury's mother.

"That's right, isn't it, dear? You stuttered so badly that you were made fun of mercilessly. You were sent away to a special school for people with congenital disabilities so that you could learn to speak clearly. It left its mark on you and made you seek perfection and revenge on the world." Pierre didn't say anything.

"Mama?" Amaury walked toward the older version of Amalie. "Why didn't you take up for Arnaud and me?" She hung her head.

"I was afraid of your father. But I'm not anymore. Come to me, son." Amaury walked over to her open arms and melted into them, crying again. "Here is your passport. Go to Texas with your boyfriend or wherever you choose. Promise me you'll be happy and stop letting your anger toward your father hold you back."

"I will." Amaury took the passport as Pierre got into the golf cart, drove off, disappearing. "We are headed for the airport and Texas. I'm afraid we must leave immediately."

"Can't you stay for the Christmas meal, my brother?" Amalie asked him.

"We must go. I want to get to Texas as soon as possible. I love you and Rawlin. Give her your mobile number to stay in touch and know when the baby is born. We have an apartment in Paris. He can give you the address, too."

Rawlin asked to see her phone, and he'd enter the contact information. She did.

After tearful goodbyes, Loren drove the men to the train station in town.

Three and a half hours later, Rawlin and Amaury heard their boarding call for New York's JFK airport where they'd change planes to DFW and then land in Lubbock, Texas, where Amaury would be introduced as Rawlin's boyfriend and love of his life.

Made in the USA
Middletown, DE
27 March 2022